Tales of
Japanese Justice

Asian Studies at Hawaii, No. 24

Tales of Japanese Justice

by Ihara Saikaku
Translated by Thomas M. Kondo *and* Alfred H. Marks

Asian Studies Program
University of Hawaii
THE UNIVERSITY PRESS OF HAWAII

Library of Congress Cataloging in Publication Data

Ihara, Saikaku, 1642–1693.
    Tales of Japanese justice.

    (Asian studies at Hawaii ; no. 24)
    Translation of Honchō ōin hiji.
    Includes bibliographical references and index.
    I. Title. II. Series.
DS3.A2A82 no. 24 [PL794] 950'.08s [895.6'3'3] 79–2566
ISBN 0–8248–0669–7

To Professor Seiji Iwata

Contents

Acknowledgments

The translators would like to thank Professor James Araki of the University of Hawaii for his valuable suggestions in revising the Introduction and the manuscript. Professor Harry Lamley, past chairman of the Asian Studies Publication Committee, University of Hawaii, and the committee members for their patience in waiting for the revision of the translation.

Finally we wish to thank Professor Isoo Munemasa of Ryūkoku University, Kyōto, Japan, for his early help and encouragement with this project.

Introduction

In his earlier years, Ihara Saikaku (1641–1693) was a *haikai* poet.¹ He excelled at speed composition and accomplished what was in his time a *Book of Records* feat of composing 23,500 verses in a single day and night. He wrote his first novel when he was forty-two (1683) and wrote many more before his death ten years later. *Tales of Japanese Justice (Honchō Ōin Hiji)* was first published in 1689, when he was forty-eight. Best known of his early prose works are fleshly pieces like *The Life of an Amorous Man (Kōshoku Ichidai Otoko)* and *Five Women Who Loved Love (Kōshoku Gonin Onna)*. The novels of his middle period were simple fables *(setsuwa): Saikaku's Tales of the Provinces (Saikaku Shokoku Monogatari), Twenty Cases of Unfilial Children in Japan (Honchō Nijū Fukō),* and *The Japanese Family Storehouse (Nihon Eitaigura),* for instance. The novels of his later years are more original works, like *Reckonings That Carry Men through the World (Seken Mune Sanyo)* and *Scraps of Letters (Yorozu no Fumi Hōgu). Tales of Japanese Justice* is a work of those mature, later years.

Donald Keene comments: "These stories have sometimes been praised as being embryonic detective stories, but they have neither suspense nor excitement, and rarely rise above the commonplace."² Though the book does not have much of the raciness generally associated with Saikaku's works, it does contain the compressed wit and ironic flashes for which the author is known. It is, in fact, a compendium of wry twists on the trial accounts popular at the time it was written. There is no principal character, except for a judge usually referred to as *gozen,* or "His Lordship," and the principal concern is very broad: justice under the Kyōto Shoshidai in the seventeenth century. Some of the stories can be traced to the *Itakura Seiyō* (Essentials of the administration of Itakura), a collection of trial records and stories of the Kyōto Shoshidai ministers Itakura Katsushige (administration from 1601–1619) and his son, Shigemune (administration from 1619–1654).

The Kyōto Shoshidai was the office of the shōgun's regional deputy in charge of imperial matters and exercising control over provincial lords; the Shoshidai maintained law and order not only in the Capital (Kyōto) but also in the surrounding provinces of Tamba (parts of present-day Kyōto and Hyōgo prefecture), Ōmi (Shiga prefecture), Harima (Hyōgo prefecture), Yamashiro (Kyōto), Yamato (Nara), Kawachi (Ōsaka), Izumi (Ōsaka), and Settsu (Ōsaka). Joseph Goedertier explains the Kyōto Shoshidai in the following way:

> (Bakufu representative in Kyōto). The name of an office of the Edo Bakufu. The word indicates a representative and was borrowed from *shoshi,* which was an office of the Muromachi Bakufu. This representative protected the imperial household but also supervised the court nobles and the daimyō who served in the capital. After the battle of Sekigahara, Okudaira Nobumasa (1555–1615), Itakura Katsushige (1545–1624), and his son Shigemune (1586–1656) were appointed *bakufu* representatives in Kyōto. For generations the daimyō hereditarily[3] held this position and were made councilors to the shōgun *(rōju).* In 1862, when the office to safeguard Kyōto (Kyōto Shugo-shoku) was created, the *Kyōto shoshidai* fell under the jurisdiction of this office.[4]

The following hierarchical graph by Masao Mitobe,[5] a law specialist, shows the administrative structure of high-ranking Bakufu officials outside the Kantō (present-day Tōkyō and the surrounding provinces) area:

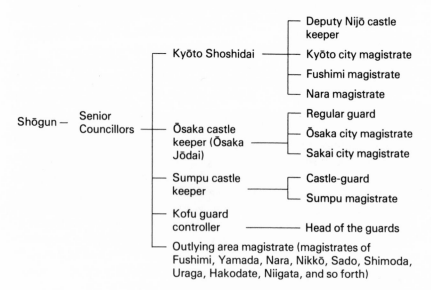

It was only a year after the decisive battle of Sekigahara that Itakura Katsushige was appointed Kyōto Shoshidai by Tokugawa Ieyasu. The Kyōto-Ōsaka area had been a stronghold of Toyotomi Hideyoshi, and Hideyoshi's heir, Hideyori, continued to wield power in Ōsaka until his ultimate defeat in the Ōsaka Summer Campaign of 1615. The difficult task of administering justice in the stronghold of the *ancien regime* is mentioned in Arai Hakuseki's *Hankanpu* (Collection of biographies and genealogies of feudal lords),[6] but Saikaku gives no direct evidence of it in *Honchō Ōin Hiji.*

From the *Hankanpu*, it is known that although Katsushige was born to a samurai family in 1545, he became an acolyte of a Zen temple in Mikawa (Aichi prefecture). When Katsushige's father and elder brother died in battle, Ieyasu, probably out of sympathy, sought him out and ordered him to renounce his priesthood so he could serve as a *gokenin* (vassal). Katsushige's thirty or so years as a Zen priest probably contributed much to the Zen-kōan telepathy displayed in his investigating methods in *Honchō Ōin Hiji.* When Ieyasu moved to Edo in 1590, he appointed Katsushige town magistrate of Edo. After a successful career of ten years in Edo, he was appointed Kyōto Shoshidai. It was a post which he tried to decline, saying that he was incapable of holding it, but Ieyasu would not take no for an answer. Katsushige accepted the post only after he had "discussed it with his wife," the *Hankanpu* records.

One of Katsushige's last acts as Kyōto Shoshidai was to execute Ieyasu's ambition of *kōbu-gattai,* uniting the emperor's family with the shōgun's family. As mediator, Katsushige placed one of the daughters of the second shōgun, Hidetada, in the imperial household of Emperor Gomizuno (reign years 1611–1629). She bore the emperor a daughter who became empress *(jotei)* in the succeeding reign, Meishō (1629–1643).

After a tenure of thirty-five years as Kyōto Shoshidai, Katsushige recommended his son, Shigemune, as successor, and retired. Like his father, his son declined the post, but the shōgun insisted again. Once in office, Shigemune refused to be outdone by his father and developed his own way of bringing precision into the judicial process. Before conducting a trial, he would make obeisance to the west, then hide himself behind a shōji door and grind tea while the court proceedings went on. No one questioned him about his peculiar behavior, and he did not bother to explain his actions until many years had passed. Then he explained that he first prayed to the deity of Atago for spiritual guidance. Then he retired behind the door to avoid being swayed by physical features into censuring or favoring someone. By the evenness of the ground tea, he knew when his heart was calm enough to make a decision on a case.

Some general statements may be made on the laws and the court system of the Tokugawa Bakufu, which, in most cases, were not universal laws extended throughout Japan. Outside of the Tokugawa domains, most provincial lords exercised fairly autonomous rule. The shōgun's *sankin-kōtai* (alternate annual attendance to the shōgun by all provincial lords) system was almost his only method of direct control.[7] In this early Tokugawa period, furthermore, most high-ranking rulers were permitted to exercise their traditional family laws *(kahō)*.

Some general statements can be made on the statutes and court systems of the Tokugawa Bakufu:[8]

1. The laws and trials were kept secret from the general populace. Law was revealed to the populace only in fragmentary public decrees *(ofuregaki)*.
2. The decision of the judge was final. (Appeals were not permitted.)
3. The judge gave the sole decision. (There were no jurors.)
4. No mediator was allowed in the trials.
5. Civil cases were settled in private as much as possible.
6. A set fee was levied on both parties regardless of who won the case. (In many cases, no fee was charged.)

Under the four-class system, it was the ruling samurai class which administered justice over farmers, artisans, and merchants. Thus samurai laws applied to all. Feuds, however, were settled in the group concerned: by family members, relatives, neighbors, guild members, or town elders (councillors).[9] Only when no mutually agreeable system could be reached were cases officially brought to court. There were district magistrates *(machi bugyō)* in most towns or cities (including, of course, Kyōto), before whom local trials were held. Trials held by the Kyōto Shoshidai minister were at the highest level (like our Supreme Court), because, although the Shoshidai was immediately below the shōgun in the Tokugawa hierarchy,[10] the shōgun no longer officiated personally at trials.

From the *Honchō Ōin Hiji,* we find that the Itakura Shoshidai ministers had time to officiate in trials even for the humblest ranks of people with their seemingly insignificant problems. For example, in Part IV, 4, "The Sickle Unreturned," a litigation is filed by a humble woodcutter because someone has stolen his sickle, the prime tool of his occupation. The Shoshidai skillfully detects the man who stole the sickle, and Saikaku writes the story with a happy ending. Though one might suspect that such an insignificant case must have been derived from the imagination of the novelist, the case is recorded in the Shoshidai's own book, *Itakura Seiyō,* as well as in Anrakuan Sakuden's *Seisuishō* (Stories to awaken people from drowsiness),[11] which even mentions the Shoshidai by name (as explained earlier, in Saikaku's novel, the Shoshidai's name is avoided in favor of a euphemistic *gozen,* or "His Lordship").

Let us look at the legal achievements of these two Shoshidai ministers, father and son, who administered the government of Kyōto and the surrounding area for over fifty years, and set the precedents which were to become "the fundamental laws of Kyōto."[12]

Itakura Katsushige promulgated the Shinshikimoku, which contained fifty-nine articles, ranging from prohibiting men and women from bathing in the same room of public bathhouses to executing sons who ignored their Neo-Confucian ethics (they were pardoned if their fathers pleaded for their sons' lives). When these laws were promulgated it is not clearly known, but Nakata has turned up strong evidence to show they were decreed between 1603 and 1612.[13]

Itakura Shigemune proclaimed the laws which came to be known as Twenty-one Furegaki,[14] covering everything from the prohibition of selling people into slavery (even the selling of daughters to the geisha quarters was prohibited unless the person being sold consented) to execution for adultery. These two judicial documents are compiled in the *Tokugawa Kinreikō,* in twelve volumes. Of course, they are also in the *Itakura Seiyō,* of which the first five chapters are devoted to the laws and the town census, and the last five chapters to actual cases of litigation. These documents are important to us as legal historical references of the Kamigata area (Kyōto and the surrounding provinces) of the early Tokugawa period.

The title of Saikaku's *Honchō Ōin Hiji* is a variation of the Chinese classic *T'ang Ying Pi Shih,* or *Trials in the Shade of a Pear Tree,* written by Kuei Wang-Jung in the thirteenth century. The word *pi shih* in Chinese (*hiji* in Japanese), not a common Japanese term, means "the comparing of things" or facts in a case. *T'ang Ying Pi Shih* has its stories in related pairs; for example, two stories about a priest who steals, with the defendant in each receiving a similar sentence. Cases were determined in the courtrooms of ancient China by precedents. The system of comparing in order to understand precedents was incorporated in Japan, but Saikaku's stories are not grouped in pairs—only his title is from the Chinese classic.[15] He has, however, borrowed at least one story from the Chinese source. Number 6 of the *T'ang Ying Pi Shih,* "Ping Chi Tests a Child," is similar to his Part I, 2 "The Cloud-clearing Shadow," which is a litigation to determine whether an old man is the father of a certain child. Saikaku perhaps incorporated this story because of its exotic method of crime detection. In it the ancient Chinese belief that the child fathered by an elderly man casts no shadow on the ground is tested in court and helps prove that the defendant is the father. The rather fantastic method of uncovering the truth used in it, however, is an exception rather than the rule.[16] Other attempts to align Saikaku's works with the *T'ang Ying Pi Shih* have not been very successful, and one can assume that most of the stories were, as avowed, Japanese.

However, it is common knowledge that the T'ang penal code was readily incorporated into Japan during the Nara and Heian periods, especially in the *ritsuryō* (*ritsu,* the criminal code; *ryō* administrative regulations in Japanese, or *lu-ling* in Chinese). The T'ang penal code, with Confucian morals as its basis, was one of the most advanced penal codes of its time. While there was much modification of these codes, the unwritten tradition of the laws remained as strong as the Confucian teachings themselves in Japan. The Neo-Confucian tradition, especially the Chu Hsi school, started to attenuate during the early Tokugawa period, but it continued to coexist with the Japanized laws, and in the social structure of Tokugawa society it often preceded legal codes. Only when there was a breach of the tradition was the legal code invoked against an offender.

This book is not, however, Saikaku's first venture into crime detection. In 1688, the year before *Honchō Ōin Hiji,* he published *Shinkashōki,* or *New Stories of Humorous Accounts* (the original *Kashōki* was written in 1642 by Joraishi). Only eight of the twenty-six stories in this book are concerned with crimes. However, Yasutaka Teruoka points out that not all the stories in the book were written by Saikaku.[17] Portions of the book are surely too poorly written to be by his hand.[18]

There are, in *Japanese Justice,* forty-four stories grouped in five parts, with more civil cases than criminal ones. The people involved are mainly commoners: merchants, artisans, and farmers. None of the cases seem to have attracted more than local notoriety.[19] In his earlier novels, however, Saikaku wrote on two famous breaches of the peace. One was the story of a young girl known as Yaoya Oshichi, burned at the stake for arson. She had started a fire which destroyed a large portion of the city of Edo, believing that the conflagration would create an opportunity for her to meet her lover again. Her story is in *Five Women Who Loved Love.* The other is the story of one of the most notorious robbers of the time, Ishikawa Goemon, who was burned to death in a caldron in 1594. His story is in *Twenty Cases of Unfilial Children in Japan.*

The criminal code of the Shoshidai was no more severe in its punishment for lawbreakers than that of any European country of this time. However, there was class distinction in Japan, and the means of execution often differed by class although the crime committed may have been similar. For example, a samurai, when found guilty of a serious offence, could still die honorably by disembowelment. Commoners could be executed by decapitation or crucifixion. There were no death penalties for priests. They were banished to far-away islands and lost their status as priests.[20]

For lesser crimes, criminals were beaten (the number of blows depended on the crime), expelled from the capital (the heavier the crime, the farther they would be expelled), disfigurement (like cutting off the nose), and tattooing. These punishments were very much like those designated in the T'ang penal codes.[21]

The punishment for manslaughter was capital punishment, but the Shoshidai showed benevolence to juveniles. This ruling dates back to the T'ang penal codes, in which a person over ninety or below seven is not held responsible for his actions. A person over eighty and below ten has limited responsibility. The law was fully applicable to those below seventy and above fifteen.[22]

One final point we must realize is that this was the age of the samurai, sworn to fight to uphold his honor. Though personal feuds were frowned upon, it was legally possible for him to kill people, especially in a vendetta. This delegation of the enforcement of justice to favored individuals (that is, the samurai) was part of Japanese culture. If the samurai proceeded through proper channels, the Shoshidai—himself a samurai—could not refuse his petition.

Japanese Justice is the prototype of crime-detection stories in Japan. Some collections which followed it are: *Honchō Tōin Hiji* (Japanese trials in the shade of a wisteria tree), published in 1707; *Ōkawa Jinseiroku* (Records of the benevolent administration of Ōkawa), published from 1854 to 1857; and *Ōoka Seidan* (Political stories of Ōoka). From the Meiji period on, novelists continued to write crime-detection stories using fictitious Edo-period characters to satisfy the readers of *taishū shōsetsu* (popular novels).

A word about the illustrations of the original woodblock publication. Saikaku, himself an artist, is said to have illustrated some of his own novels, in particular, *The Life of a Man Who Lived for Love* and *Saikaku's Tales from the Provinces*.[23] Through Futō Mizutani's research, however, it is known that the artist of *Honchō Ōin Hiji* was Hambei Yoshida, who lived in Kyōto about 1665 to 1690. He is said to have illustrated about half of Saikaku's *ukiyo-zōshi*. *Honchō Ōin Hiji* has thirteen two-page woodblock illustrations and eight one-page woodblock illustrations. There is no picture of "His Lordship," because it was not only disrespectful to draw pictures of such a high-ranking statesman but illegal, though lower-ranking law officials are depicted (wearing swords and carrying cudgels).

Previous Translations of *Honchō Ōin Hiji*

Morisawa, Saburō, *Saikaku's Short Stories,* in *The Reeds* (Kansai University of Foreign Studies), March, 1955, Volume 1, III, 4 of *Honchō Ōin Hiji.*

Morisawa, Saburō, *Feudal Tales of Detection,* in *The Reeds* (Kansai University of Foreign Studies), March, 1956, Volume 2, I, 4; II, 4: and IV, 9.

Munemasa, Isoo and Kondō, Thomas M., *A Short Bow of the Jyuya-Nembutsu,* in *Kokubungaku-ronsō* (Ryūkoku University), November, 1967, Volume 13, II, 1 of *Honchō Ōin Hiji.*

Munemasa, Isoo, and Kondō, Thomas M., *Japanese Trials Under the Shade of a Cherry Tree,* in *Ryūkoku daigaku ronshū* (Ryūkoku University), August, 1968, Volume 386, I, 1–8 of *Honchō Ōin Hiji.*

NOTES

1. A type of humorous poem.
2. Donald Keene, *World within Walls* (New York: Holt, Rinehart and Winston, 1976), p. 202.
3. Goedertier's statement needs clarification. One had to be a *daimyō* to hold this post, but it was not strictly hereditary.
4. Joseph Goedertier, *A Dictionary of Japanese History* (Tōkyō: Weatherhill, 1968).
5. Masao Mitobe, *Nihonshi gaisetsu shiryō* [Outline documents on Japanese history] (Tōkyō: Meigetsushobō, 1964), pp. 183–184.
6. Written in 1701 and published in Tōkyō by Yoshikawa Kobunkan in 1925.
7. See Toshio Tsukahira, *Feudal Control in Tokugawa Japan, The Sankin Kōtai System* (Boston, Massachusetts: Harvard University Press, 1970).
8. Kingo Kobayakawa, *Kinsei minji soshō seido no kenkyū* [A study of the civil litigation system in the recent era](Tōkyō: Yūhikaku, 1957), p. 67.
9. See Dan F. Henderson, *Conciliation and Japanese Law, Tokugawa and Modern* (Seattle, Washington: University of Washington, 1965). Also see John H. Wigmore, *Law and Justice in Tokugawa Japan,* 10 vols. (Tōkyō: University of Tōkyō Press, 1969 onward).
10. Conrad Totman, *Politics in the Tokugawa Bakufu, 1600–1843* (Boston, Massachusetts: Harvard University Press, 1967), p. 41.
11. A collection of amusing stories by the inventor of *rakugo* (humorous storytelling). Sakuden collaborated with the Itakura Shoshidai.
12. *Nihon rekishi daijiten,* vol. 1, ''Kyōto shoshidai'' (Tōkyō: Kawade shobo, 1956).
13. Masajirō Takigawa, *Nihon hōseishi,* p. 395.
14. In the compilation of the *Tokugawa Kinreikō,* 6, there is no title to this statute, and there are actually twenty-two articles.
15. Isoji Asō, *Ihara Saikaku-shū* 2 (Tōkyō), pp. 358–359.

16.   In our present-day scientific society, this belief seems ridiculous, but belief in it has been recorded as fact in Terashima's *Wakan Sansai-zue,* an illustrated encyclopedia of those days.

17.   Taizō Ebara, *et al., Teihon Saikaku zenshū* (Tōkyō: Chūō Kōron, 1959), pp. 8–9.

18.   The pen name *Saikaku* was illegal from 1688 to 1691 because its second character (*kaku,* or *tsuru,* meaning 'crane') was closely associated with the ruling Tokugawa family. The *Shin-kashōki* was therefore published under the name Saihō (the character for *hō,* or 'phoenix', resembles the proscribed *kaku*).

19.   With the possible exception of the incident of persecution of Christians in Kyōto, consult Isoo Munemasa, "Daiusu-chō to Oranda Saikaku" [Deus town and the Dutch Saikaku], in *Saikaku no Kenkyū* (Tōkyō: Miraisha, 1969), pp. 96–111. Though Saikaku does not explicitly refer to the Christian persecution, the story "The Short Bow of the Ten-night Nembutsu" seems related to it.

20.   Kobayakawa, *Kinsei minji soshō seido no kenkyū,* p. 119.

21.   What seems to be missing in Japan were the punishments by castration and fines which were common in T'ang.

22.   Noboru Niida, *Chūgoku hōseishi kenkyū, hō to kaishaku* [A study on the Chinese law system, law and its interpretation] (Tōkyō), p. 22.

23.   Ivan Morris, trans., *The Life of an Amorous Woman* (New York: New Directions Books, 1963), p. 45.

Part I
WISDOM

1. Mount Matsuba
   in Early Spring[1]

In T'ang China, the flower was the pear blossom, and in the shade of that tree Shao Kung Shih carried out justice.[2] Poems have been written about it. In Japan, the flower is the cherry blossom, and countless poems have been composed in its shade. In Our Majesty's reign, the mountains stand unwavering; the four ocean plains lie quiet under never varying, tranquil waves. Purely flow the waters of the Imperial Capital,[3] never to cease their flow.

In the Capital, there once lived an elderly sage, one of an illustrious line. He did not need a cane until he was past one hundred, and he listened to the stories as if he heard evil with one ear and good with the other. These stories have amused many in our time and calmed hearts blown about like bush clover and miscanthus in the winds of emotion. Unfortunately all of them could not be written down by a forest of brushes; so I have had to leave some out.

Long ago, in one of the neighborhoods of the Capital, lived a man who arranged traditional observances for a very high-ranking family.[4] Every year on December twenty-first he would go to a certain village on the border of Tamba Province,[5] and there on the mountain would cut pines to be used for New Year's decorations.[6]

There was one village on the eastern edge of that mountain and another village on the western edge, and every year the village masters of the two villages would meet and argue endlessly about which village owned the mountain. One of the village masters would bring out an old scroll that he said set forth the right of his village to cut from the so-called Decoration Mountain. Then he would say, "Therefore the mountain is under the jurisdiction of my village." The other village master would bring out another scroll which did not differ from the other by so much as a single word or punctuation mark and make the same claim for his village. The matter was very difficult to solve.

On that mountain, close to the beautiful peak, stood a camphorwood, one-*ken*-square shrine sacred to the bodhisattva Kannon. It was said to have been built in the Daidō era (806–818 A.D.). The door to its inner sanctum had been nailed shut long ago, and no one prayed before it. No lights flickered there, and no pilgrims ever appeared. It had become a fine resting place for woodcutters. The main altar was buried under leaves.

The dispute over the mountain finally came before His Lordship in the form of a dispute between the two villages over the ownership of that Kannon shrine.[7] His Lordship summoned both village masters to Kyōto and said, "There must be a reason that each village has the same record, and that the scrolls do not mention the Kannon shrine. It seems likely to me that they were recorded after the Daidō era. Tell me, what kind of Kannon image is it? Of course, if it is an esoteric image, nobody has seen it, but just the same I would think there are rumors about it. At any rate, I shall award the shrine to the one who knows what it is."

After pondering the matter, one village master said, "It is exactly like the Thousand-hand Kannon of Kiyomizu temple."[8] The other village master thought for a while with his cheek on his fist and said, "It is the Nyoirin Kannon, the one with her finger to her cheek."[9] His Lordship noted the replies and then dispatched officers to open the shrine. When they opened the door, they slapped their hands together in amazement. It was not Kannon but a ferocious lightning deity bound in chains; just a glance at him was enough to make one shudder.

When the investigating officers returned to Kyōto and reported their findings, His Lordship did not seem very surprised. He simply summoned all the craftsmen of Buddhist images in the Capital, described the image to them, and then said, "Has any of you ever heard of the carving of such an image?"

A great craftsman of Buddhist images, one Hokkyō Minbu, who lived in Gojō, produced a scroll of his family business bearing a notation showing that his ancestors of six generations earlier had carved the image in question. He explained:

According to this scroll, during the night of heavy snowfall on November 18, 1394—that was during the reign of the Emperor Gokomatsu[10]— countless bolts of lightning shattered trees and destroyed homes in the two villages by Decoration Mountain. Twenty-four men and women lost their lives, and the people were weighed down with grief, but an itinerant priest of the Shingon sect appeared from the northern provinces and brought the lightning under control.

After that, not even the year's first lightning, that which awakens the insects from hibernation, was heard; so the happy villagers built and worshipped an image of the lightning deity and prayed it would be enshrined there for years to come. Now, when they prayed for rain, there was always a good response. As the years went by, I suppose, the villagers forgot the incident. Proof that my ancestors built the image, however, may be found, the scroll tells me, in a document left inside the pedestal.

Men were sent to investigate the pedestal and found there a scroll confirming everything Hokkyō Minbu had said. It was signed by the heads of the two villages. One was the father-in-law of the other.

"It seems to me," said His Lordship, "that this document must have been made up by one of the village masters, who then gave a duplicate copy to the other. You villagers, it is clear, were related long ago, and there is no reason why you should not be now. From now on, therefore, work this matter out among yourselves, using the shrine as the boundary between the east and the west sides of the mountain. When you cut the pine trees to decorate the twelve gates of the Imperial Palace,[11] be sure to follow the tradition of cutting twelve from each side."

Thus it was harmoniously settled that the mountain and its pine trees would go on for a thousand years or even eight thousand years without change.

2. The Cloud-clearing Shadow

Long ago, in one of the neighborhoods of the Capital, there lived a canny lumber merchant. The ground under the eaves of his home were piled high with lumber from Mount Kiso to be used for summer cottages. He had been adept at business since his youth, and his storehouse like the pine would endure a thousand years.[1] His wealth would continue flowing in the generations of his grandchildren and his great grandchildren even if they made no effort to replenish it. And yet the man, even now past eighty, made no effort to turn over his fortune to his son.[2] He took great joy in counting his wealth at the end of each year. His head was combed with frost, on his forehead the waves never stopped breaking, his back was like an arched bridge.

"In this world so hard to cross," people began to say, "how silly it is for him to work so hard. If he dies now, he will probably be seized by devils and carried away in a flaming coach."[3] He heard people saying this, then he heard the sound of the drum calling the faithful to the 2 P.M. mass, and he hastened tardily to the temple to pray for the repose of his soul in the life hereafter.

People laughed at this. Of course, what he was doing was a good thing. He had taken bodhi into his heart and had turned to the religious life.[4] His new self was as different from the old as heaven is from earth.

"Earth" and "Sky" were the names written on a pair of his chests,[5] one character on each chest. He placed in them a thousand kamme of silver to be passed on to his son. Then he made plans to retire to the vicinity of Okazaki,[6] to a house built of the lumber from Saga he had been saving. The shutters of his windows there swung outward so he could see the mountains. How happy he was there in his declining years, regretting only that he had not abandoned his worldly life earlier!

Since his wife had died twenty years before, he did not feel lonely in his monkish life. His son was a good man and executed his filial duties piously. Every day he brought his father the first foods picked.[7] He hired four or five beautiful maids to serve his father, but the old man drew the line at letting them lay out his bed. He acted so much like one in a charcoal robe who had left the world that the maids' hearts were uplifted.

As the years passed, however, a homely kitchen maid suddenly began growing strangely stouter. When people spoke to her about it with knowing smiles, she named her employer. She was criticized harshly for suggesting such a terrible thing, and the old man, told of it, said he would not have done it even in his dreams.

The maid was discharged from the household, and while waiting for reemployment gave birth to a baby boy.[8] She nursed the baby with care, and when the period of pollution was over sought to place the child in the household of her former master, but no one would have anything to do with her.[9] Not knowing what else to do, she ran with the baby in her arms into the magistrate's mansion and sorrowfully told her story.

The old man was summoned to court and interrogated by His Lordship. He answered, "I don't know anything about it."

Then His Lordship said, "Both of you report here again tomorrow morning, the fourteenth."

When the parties returned the next morning, His Lordship explained, "In T'ang China, there was a case resembling this one. When a child fathered by a man over eighty is placed in the sun, he casts no shadow.[10] If this child casts no shadow, the old man is undoubtedly his father."

They stood the baby up in the courtyard, and, lo and behold, he threw no shadow. The old man was at a loss for explanations and said, "I attempted to conceal the truth out of fear of the criticism of society. He is indeed my son."

Then the mother of the child pleaded that the child's future be provided for, but she was told by the magistrate: "Such a child cannot survive for more than a hundred days. If he lives beyond that period, you may plead your case in court again." With this verdict, the parties left the court.

The old man, however, felt pity for the child and had him cared for day and night. But unfortunately the child grew gradually weaker until, true to the prediction of His Lordship, he died, it is said, ninety-seven days after his birth.

3. In The Ear
The Same Word Resounds

Long ago in a part of the Capital, there was a tea store called Nishi no Okaya. The proprietor had left his birthplace and come here thirteen years earlier, and was finally realizing how different was the life of the merchant from the life of hoe, plow, and cow his family had known for many generations. His funds had diminished year by year, and he was no longer able to make a living. He had to change his livelihood once more.

It was difficult to raise money in the Capital, so he thought of the rice paddies willed to him by his parents, now in the care of relatives, and decided to sell them. When he spoke to his relatives in the village about his plan, they, who would do anything out of greed, banded together and informed him they had bought the land from him. No, they had not been simply entrusted with it.

He asked them, "Do you have a bill of sale?"

They asked him, "Do you have a certificate to show you left the land with us?"

"They are thieves," he thought. "They are close relatives, so naturally I did not require any documents. I regret that now, but there is nothing I can do about it. I shall not, however, accept it without protest. I shall prepare a brief and file suit."

The farmer's relatives were summoned, and the trial began. The spokesman for the farmers noisily remonstrated: "Uncle, do not accuse us when you have no proof."

The man from the Capital angrily replied, "Uncle, if my accusations were without grounds, would I take them before His Lordship?"

The word "uncle" used by both parties caught in His Lordship's ears. "Let us forget the trial," he said; "you people are no better than beasts. If your grandfather were alive now he would be punished as a criminal. We shall proceed no further with this case; you must settle it in private. If you continue to contravene the laws that hold men together, your genealogy will be written up and posted where the people of the Capital can see it."

The officers in attendance marveled at this verdict of His Lordship, because though they had pondered the case, they could find no solution. Yet His Lordship understood instantly what must have happened to make an heir his uncle's uncle:

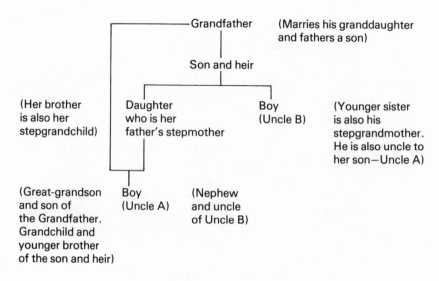

(Uncles A and B are involved in the litigation)

4. They Did Not Know What Was in the Drum

Long ago as now the part of the Capital known as Nishijin was the weaving district,[1] and there the houses of the silk weavers stood gate to gate vying for customers. In one of them lived the weaver Ōno, a good man and a fine weaver, though he did not prosper. Finally, sadly, he and his wife decided they must sell all their possessions and leave for other parts.

Word got around that he was quietly selling his belongings, and ten of his friends, also members of the weavers' guild, gathered together to discuss the problem. "He is a good businessman," said one, "he never does anything shady, his faith in Buddha and the gods never wavers, he is of upright character, and he is always trying to help others." All agreed they did not want to lose their friend. They decided to assist him in paying his debts so that he could go on with his business. When they inquired as to his indebtedness, they learned that he owed the rather small sum of four *kamme*.[2]

"Are you leaving the business you have maintained so long only for this? This is nothing. In fact, it could happen to anyone," said one of his friends. "Let us take care of everything. Forget your troubles and have a good time getting ready for the New Year. Make *mochi* flowers for your children and make them happy. Give your employees new robes, though it might be well to spare the addition of the family crests and make them a light color so they can be redyed."

Another one of the friends said to his wife: "Don't be so glum! Put up your hair and look as if nothing has happened. Here, have one of these fresh-caught *buri* (fish) for your evening meal. See, I still have two."

On December twenty-sixth, always a busy night, the ten friends came to his home; each of them had ten *ryō* of gold coins. They dropped their contributions in a barrel and made up what is called a *tanomoshi* fund.[3] It amounted to 100 *ryō*.

"It will soon be a thousand," said one of the friends, as he placed the barrel on the altar of the god Ebisu.[4] "Neighbor Daikoku,"[5] he giggled, speaking to that god, "strike your hammer again and again. If you don't I'll send you down the Kamiya River." Then they began drinking *sake,* and since everyone was cheerful, even the man in debt grew lighthearted.

"This is an unforgettable New Year's eve," he said as the nondrinkers as well as the drinkers lost their sense with wine. They took turns dancing; they said things they forgot later, and when it was time to depart, they put on each other's sandals, forgot their overcoats, dropped their fans, and left without saying proper goodbyes. The 4 A.M. chimes had rung and the roosters were crowing as they left the house.

Worn out by the evening's festivities, the host supported his head against a box of dishes. His wife locked the gates more carefully than usual and sent the servants to bed. Then, bursting with joy, she shook her husband, saying, "Let's look at our accounts," and took out the account book and an abacus.

The man awoke and said, "This New Year's I'll give the bill collectors a hard time when the gold is weighed. And wait till I see the rice dealer Yaemon. He's been the worst, even though he's our relative. We'll pay off our bills and beginning this New Year's day will pay everything in cash." Figures danced through his head as he took the barrel down from the altar, but when he looked inside it the money was gone.

The husband and wife were dumbfounded. "They were hard gold coins; surely a rat couldn't have carried them off. Did the gods hide them?" They searched the altar over and over but in the end could only conclude the money was gone.

Now they felt worse than ever. "It must be our fate," he said. "The thief is not to blame; let us not hate him. And yet what a terrible thing has been done to us! Here we accepted help without thinking what it might mean and we find we have only caused ourselves trouble. What will people think? We will not be able to live with it. Let us do away with our children and ourselves.''

His wife was suddenly calm. "How true," she said; "we have nothing to live for." She began to change into a white robe,[6] saying, "People will look at our bodies." Then she sat before a mirror and combed her hair more sumptuously than usual and caressed her husband's hair, saying, "Indeed, the love we have known for these nineteen years is like a dream of dawn." Her eyes were filled with tears.

Then she lit the family altar and woke her two children. One child asked, "Is today the day we are going to make *mochi* flowers?" His brother, sleepy though he was, remembered his magic bow. The wife kept staring at them and weeping until a maid who had been with the family for a long time became aware of what was going on. She asked no questions but simply began to wail in a loud voice.

"You parents may well have good reason to do this, but must you take the lives of innocent children?" she asked. Then she pleaded: "Please be reasonable. Let me bring the children up myself." Her entreaties became so loud that before long she awoke everyone in the household. When dawn broke on the horizon, all thoughts of suicide had been abandoned.

A few of the weaver friends soon heard of the incident and informed the others who had been at the party. They all conferred on the matter but were at a loss for a solution. Surely, they felt, someone who helped in a matter of this kind would not steal the proceeds. And yet the thief could not have come from the outside.

Someone said, "Let us have a trial by hot steel[7]; then we can clear ourselves."

A more prudent man said, "That will not solve the matter."

Finally they said, "Let us take this case to His Lordship and leave everything to his judgment."

A statement was prepared and sent to His Lordship. His answer was: "We have no time to take care of this matter this year; it will interfere with the business of all concerned. Let us, then, go into it on the 25th of January. In the meantime, do not any of you leave the Capital." The weavers received the order and returned home.

After New Year's Day, the ten men were ordered to appear before the court with their wives. "If you have no wife," the order said, "bring a sister or a niece, but without fail bring a woman." Although the men were annoyed, they all reported to the court as ordered. There they drew lots to determine the order each couple would be taken in the days to come.

Each day thereafter one of the couples was asked to carry a large Chinese drum suspended from a long pole all the way from the mansion of His Lordship west around Miya-no-Matsubara and back. Spectators were kept at a distance. This went on for ten days, until all the couples had made the trip as a punishment for losing the *tanomoshi* fund.

The residents of the Capital who saw them were amazed. "What an unusual punishment!" they said. None so much as imagined that a small, shrewd priest was sitting inside the drum!

After ten days the priest reported to His Lordship: "Every woman complained, but the wife who carried the drum on the eighth day was the most resentful. She said, 'You gave your share. How can they do this to us? Is it our fate to suffer like this?' Her husband whispered to her, 'Just bear it a little longer. It's not easy to steal a hundred *ryō* of gold.' "

The man was called up and severely interrogated. In the end, he told the authorities where to find the stolen money. It was returned to the loser, who received it with great joy.

Later, the sentence was passed: "Though you are a thief, since you were one of the ten contributors your life will be spared. You will, however, be banished from the Capital." Then, it is said, the husband and wife were driven out, one to the east, the other to the west.

5. The Wonderful Potion That Calls One's Name

A long time ago in the Capital, there lived a man who had come over the sea from Sado Island and taken up residence in Gojō Shiogama-machi.[1] He lived a bachelor's existence in a rented home. He had one servant, who did the kitchen work, who had accompanied him from Sado.

He was a man of simple needs, who could live comfortably on only eight hundred *me* of silver, and he thought to himself: "There is nobody as free of care as I. This year I am past the age of fifty, and even if I am blessed with long life I only have to worry about supporting myself twenty years more. I can rely on others about as much as a monkey who falls from a tree,[2] but after all I have neither parent to look after nor child with a future to worry about. I brought twenty-five hundred pieces of gold with me from Sado, so at present I have sufficient funds to see me through two hundred years. I don't know what it is like to be extravagant, and I have nothing to spend my money on save tickets to dramatic performances. I still haven't found any friends who are likely to take me to the geisha quarters. After living here for over half a year, I have decided there is really not much going on even in the Capital."

There was another man in the same rooming house who had no stable occupation, but thanks to the favors of the sons of rich families in the Capital passed an existence that was little more than a dream. Night was day for him; he led a life that knew no bounds. Only in the Capital would he have been permitted to live as he did. He rarely used his stove, so his neighbors did not have to worry about fire starting in his room—that was the only good thing they could say for him.

Somehow this man learned that his Sado neighbor was wealthy. He immediately cast about for ways to gain his favor. He finally won the trust of the Sado man and proceeded to introduce him to the geisha quarters of Rokujō and into the company of the prosperous sons of Kyōto. After leading him into a frolic with the queen courtesan, he recommended his friend to five young men anxious to borrow money at any rate, even seventy percent a month. "This country fellow is loaded!" He carried their petitions to the Sado man, who immediately complied.

"I have enough money, fortunately," he said. "I will lend each of them five hundred *ryō;* that makes twenty-five hundred *ryō.*" Then he made a condition: "Since this gold is to see me through life, will you take turns returning the amount I need each year for my personal expenses? If I die before the loan is paid, I have no one to will the unpaid balance to, so, in that event, would you be so good as to give me a memorial service?" His spirit of detachment was like that of one who loans money that has rained from heaven. They were very grateful, and sure they would not forget their promises.

Thus the country man was emancipated from the fear that his money might be stolen from his room. He began to visit the geisha quarters more frequently, at times to spend the night.

One exceptionally chilly night somewhere in the middle of November, when they were pursuing their nightly pleasures, the man who had ingratiated himself with the country man, and had cherished evil thoughts against him from the beginning, thought to himself: "If I kill this man, the five men who borrowed from him will gain much, and I will receive great reward from them." Avarice flooded over him; he slipped poison into the intoxicated Sado man's wine. They were at the geisha quarters at the time, but the Sado man did not feel ill until he returned home.

He was unable to move his body and lay mumbling incoherently. His servant, filled with concern, hurried to report the case to His Lordship while his master was still alive. He produced the promissory note and said, "These are the people my master was with last night."

The five men, as well as all the others who had been in the room with the sick man, were summoned; interrogation was carried out in various ways, but because the Sado man was in a daze, it was difficult to single out the culprit. His Lordship pondered for a while and then summoned his family physician. The physician advised: "As an experiment, let the man drink this amazing potion that has been handed down from the past. It is made from tinder produced from the head of an old drum. When the potion enters his stomach, it is claimed, he will name the one who made him drink the poison. This is written in the medical books of China, so let us behold this marvel. Watch!"

Some people observed in awe; others said, skeptically, "What's this?" Everyone listened carefully as the sick man began to move his lips, and from his throat could be heard the name: "Moroku, Moroku, the fool." All were amazed. Moroku was placed under arrest, and after being interrogated he confessed his crime. Then, it is said, he was executed.

6. Twins Who Break a Blood Tie

A long time ago, in the Capital, lived a pharmacist whose sign announced: "A wondrous drug, handed down through a single son, a drug given power by the gods to cure all illnesses." His name was known in the suburbs as well as the Capital, and his shop in Shijō was famous. He was over fifty years old and regretted not having a son to inherit his estate. Then, just when he learned to his joy that his wife would bear him a child, he passed away. Before the thirty-fifth day of mourning,[1] his wife had a normal delivery that was nevertheless different from most births. She produced twins—in fact, sons.

Out of concern for the fatherless children, whom she named Umematsu and Takematsu, the mother gave them to wet nurses to be reared. Then, during the summer of their thirteenth year, she died. How sad is this impermanent world. The sons had only each other and the foster mothers—there were no other kin.

Each foster mother, however, felt that the son she was rearing should be the heir. Their arguments went on without end. Finally, against the advice of the elders of the neighborhood, they entered into litigation.

The head clerk,[2] who had worked in this household for many years, filed a third claim: "If this house is divided in half, its slogan, 'handed down through a single son,' will be invalid; that will hurt more than the division of the estate. One son should inherit the home and business; the other should be compensated with a legacy of equal value and be adopted into another family."[3]

The clerk's view was given great weight, and an old midwife of Kyōto, named "Crinkled Hair," was called in and asked: "When twin sons are born, which is the elder—the one born first or the one born second?"

"Judging by old cases of the kind I know of," she quavered, "the one born second should be named the heir of the home. That is because he was closer to his mother in the womb, and his relationship to her is closer. The one born first is the one in back, so he even gets the breast last, and his body is a little smaller."

When the son who was born second, Takematsu, was about to be named the inheritor of the family name, the foster mother of Umematsu was obdurate. "His mother had a reason for naming him Umematsu. Everyone knows his name means the 'elder brother of flowers.' I believe every single thing in the household should be divided fairly," she said.

His Lordship found the suggestions of the head clerk most appropriate, but he permitted Umematsu's foster mother to have her way. "Let us divide everything in half," he said.

Then he inquired what religious sect the family belonged to. He was told: "All the generations of the family, down to the humblest servant, have always belonged to the Nichiren sect."

"If so, open the family altar and bring me the altar image," he ordered. When the image of Saint Nichiren was brought in, he said: "We shall start now to divide the household goods. The two foster mothers should each grasp this image and break it exactly in half." Then His Lordship left the courtroom.

"How can we do that, for any reason?" The foster mothers said. "We cannot break the Buddha to whom we have prayed for life hereafter." With that, these two people who had refused to listen to the advice of their townspeople came to their senses and for the first time regretted having precipitated so needless a dispute.

Both foster mothers then requested that matters should be carried out as the head clerk had suggested; they agreed that Umematsu was the younger brother and that Takematsu should inherit the home. They also decided they would settle the division of the household goods out of court. When they announced their decision to His Lordship, he gave them permission to proceed in this way. Thus the case was settled.

7. Nine Drinks of Sake— and Living

Long ago in the Capital, an artisan who lived in Teramachi devised Japan's first ten-drink *sake* cup.[1] It was said to be not inferior in ingenuity to the cup created by Yen Shih,[2] in China. Day and night he revelled, drinking *sake,* toying with his cup, until he fell ill and, after some time, finally died, leaving two sons, ages eighteen and fifteen. After the hundred days of mourning was past, his home was searched in the presence of town councillors, but no will could be found.

An inventory was made of all the gold, silver, and household goods. Then the brothers were told: "According to the laws of society, the elder brother should receive 60 percent of the wealth, and the younger should have 40 percent. Finally, both brothers should observe proper filial piety to their mother."

The younger brother, however, refused to accept this counsel. "I want half of the home and half of everything else," he said.

"If so," the town councillors said, "your brother's seniority will go unrecognized." They tried to reason with him, but when he would not accede it became a case for His Lordship.

His Lordship listened to the various pleas and said: "The advice of the town councillors is most reasonable. If you have a good reason for claiming half, speak out."

"The reason I should be treated as the oldest child even though my brother was born before I was is that, I am ashamed to say, my mother was only my father's maid when she conceived my brother. My father's relatives intervened to make her his legal wife. My birth, however, was entirely legitimate. Thus, although I am the younger brother, since I was born legitimately I should be treated as the elder brother and heir. Such a practice is commonly followed in the homes of samurai."

"He has a point there," said His Lordship, "but was the home purchased when the mother was a maid, or more recently?"

"It was purchased when she was a maid," said one of the town councillors.

"Then," ordered His Lordship, "as the younger brother wishes, the fortune shall be divided in half. The older brother, however, is awarded the home, and as the heir there he will take care of his mother."

8. A Gift of a False Sleeve

A long time ago in a town of the Capital, there lived a man who dealt in Chinese and domestic silks. He was shrewd in business and accumulated two thousand *kamme,* but then, just when his shop had reached the peak of its prosperity, he died. He was forty-two years old.[1]

All his wealth was willed to his daughter, then two years old. Her mother, a widow of thirty-three,[2] cut her hair and retreated from this floating world. She prayed for the day when her child would become an adult and, abandoning all thought of another marriage, entered the path to buddhahood. She turned over all her former business responsibilities to relatives, deposited all her gold and silver in a bank, and reduced her household staff to seven. She had all she wished.

One day she and the members of her household went to view the blossoms at Higashiyama. They left no one to look after the house but locked the gates. When they returned home at dusk, however, they saw someone in one of the living rooms. They all shouted, in surprise: "A robber, in broad daylight."

They cornered the intruder and quickly captured him, and then discovered that he was the son of the neighbor on the south side. He was seventeen and still wore his hair in the adolescent *sumi-maegami* style.[3] The town councillors who were called in found the matter so delicate they decided not to press charges against him, but the youth stepped forward and said, "I had the widow's permission to be here." All present looked at the widow with suspicion in their eyes. They were at a loss for words.

Tears flowed from the widow's eyes. "Oh my," she said, "how terrible to be suspected of something of which you are innocent. He is a son I would not be ashamed to call my own, but if he were really guilty of what he says, he would not have been able to confess it. I will find the truth of the matter, though, even if my body should be cut into eight parts in the process." Then she said to herself, "A woman has her own way of settling things."

Deaf to the advice of those about her, she went to His Lordship and told him what had happened. The young man was called in. "If you had secret relations with the widow," His Lordship said, "produce the love letters you received. If you cannot show us any love letters we can trace to the widow, you will be charged with burglary."

The young man said, "It was all done secretly; I burned each letter immediately after reading it."

"If so you will have to be punished. Don't you have any evidence at all?" said His Lordship.

The young man pondered awhile and then brazenly began taking off his clothes and showed his underwear—a blue, short-sleeved garment bearing a crest of three butterflies. "This is the widow's undergarment," he said, with tears in his eyes. "She put it around me when I left her one windy night. She also gave me an ornamental comb and a perfume container. I cannot understand how she can give me such things and then accuse me of burglary."

The objects were examined, and the garment and crest were found to be identical with the widow's. Then His Lordship said to her, "Did you give him the short-sleeved garment?"

The widow was silent for a time and then said, "Out of fear of what people would say, I have been attempting to conceal our relationship, but now it is revealed. Perhaps fate has decreed it. It is true that I have been intimate with this man."

"Then you are a criminal who has needlessly upset society by giving frivolous testimony," said His Lordship. "Such is the vain heart of woman. Stand up."

The youth, head down, spoke up: "There is something I would like to confess. The widow has said this was an illicit relationship; that is not true. It was I who lied. My extreme youth has led me to squander a large part of my father's wealth, and recently I was on the verge of being disowned. My relatives, however, intervened, and I was forgiven after only an apology to my father.

"Yet I lost my freedom. Then I suddenly remembered the widow, my wealthy neighbor, and decided to enter her house and steal something. In case I was caught and interrogated, I had this short-sleeved garment made in imitation of hers to save myself. I plotted it all; I am guilty," he said.

His Lordship listened to the confession and then said: "First of all, let me say how I admire the spirit of this widow. She had the courage to bear the disgrace and sacrificed herself. She lied about an illicit relationship in order to save him. In this broad Capital, there is no woman like her."

His Lordship kept talking about the compassionate heart of the woman: "She is the paragon of all women, a heart without a flaw. Hereafter her relatives should take even better care of her."

Then, to the young man, His Lordship said, "Your crimes are many, and you should be punished, but moved by the heart of the widow, just when you were about to be freed, you repented and admitted your guilt.

You unhesitatingly acted to save the widow.'' The young man was thus commended, and though ordinarily he would have been executed, his life was spared and, it is said, he was expelled from the Capital.

NOTES TO PART I

1. MOUNT MATSUBA IN EARLY SPRING

In *Itakura Seiyō,* Book VII, 8, ''On the Feud over a Place to Cut Grass,'' two villages in Tamba engage in a dispute over a piece of property. Though the case is not the same, the beginning resembles Saikaku's.

1. Early spring, January. Spring was the first three months of the year.
2. Shao Kung Shih, or Shōhaku in Japanese. A statesman of the Chou dynasty (1122–255 B.C.), his capable administration is hailed in the poem classic *Shih Ching,* or the Book of Odes.
3. Kyōto, where the emperor resided; however, the Tokugawa shogunate was in Edo (Tōkyō).
4. Man, *Toshi-otoko,* literally, ''year-man.'' His duty was to take care of ceremonial duties of nobles.
5. Tamba province at present is part of northern Kyōto and Hyōgo prefecture.
6. The pine symbolizes longevity because it is an evergreen.
7. His Lordship, or the judges of the trials, were assumed to be Kyōto Shoshidai ministers.
8. The Thousand-hand Kannon is called *Avalokitesvara* in Sanskrit and *Kuan Yin* in Chinese. This bodhisattva (a stage before becoming a buddha) can change into thirty-three different forms; but in many statues, the bodhisattva is depicted in feminine form. Its multiple hands are to save beings in various ways.
9. Nyoirin Kannon is *Cintamanicakra* in Sanskrit. This bodhisattva is depicted in a thinking position with a finger of its right hand on its cheek.
10. Emperor Gokomatsu, Emperor of the Northern Dynasty, after victory over the Southern Dynasty, in 1392, became the sole emperor.
11. Twelve gates of the Kyōto Imperial Palace is meant, however, there seems to be no record of such an Imperial Household custom.

2. THE CLOUD-CLEARING SHADOW

In *T'ang Ying Pi Shih,* No. 6, ''Ping Chi Tests a Child,'' a man had a daughter who left the home when married. The man's wife died, so he remarried, though past eighty. After fathering a son, the man died. The daughter of the first wife claimed the inheritance, saying that the son was not by her father. The judge, Ping Chi, had a way to test this: the son fathered by an old man always feels cold and casts no shadow on the ground. The daughter was punished for causing unnecessary litigation.

1. A storehouse or vault for household valuables and money was long an architectural requisite of the wealthy Japanese home.
2. His son. During the Tokugawa Period, it was the common practice to retire at forty-five, at which time the home was bequeathed to the eldest son.
3. Devils were the custodians of *jigoku,* the Buddhist hell.
4. *Bodhi,* holiness.

5.   The boxes were grouped in pairs with these names. Each box contained 10 *kamme* (about 82.6 pounds) of silver.

6.   Okazaki is located in present-day Sakyō Ward, at the foot of Higashiyama. During the seventeenth century it was the outskirts of the Capital, where many wealthy people lived in retirement.

7.   This refers to the belief that one lives seventy-five days longer each time one eats the first picked foods of the day.

8.   While waiting for reemployment servants lived in an employment agency until they were hired. These were called *koyado* or *hōkōnin-yado*.

9.   A period of pollution was called *imi,* the period of childbirth was thought to be a polluted period, and for a certain period after childbirth, parents and newborn would avoid association with other people. Among commoners, the periods of pollution were: seven days for a father, thirty-five days for a mother, thirty-one days for a baby boy, and thirty-three days for a baby girl. In this story, it must have been after the thirty-sixth day.

10.   Such a belief may have been accepted at this time. This belief is also set forth in volume 8 of the *Wakan Sansai Zue,* an illustrated encyclopedia published in 1715.

3. IN THE EAR THE SAME WORD RESOUNDS

Professor Teiji Takita points out a similar story in *Tōin Hiji Genkai,* a Japanese commentary on the *T'ang Ying Pi Shih,* No. 121, "Ch'uan Lung's Decision on Family Relationship." Grandmother Ch'ao kills her daughter-in-law, Yu-tzu. Yu-tzu's son, Ch'eng, seeks vengeance but is deterred by the judge, Ch'uan Lung, who points out that he would be harming his mother's mother. It is not an illicit relationship as in Saikaku's tale.

4. THEY DID NOT KNOW WHAT WAS IN THE DRUM

In *T'ang Ying Pi Shih,* No. 18, "Tao Jang Uses a Prisoner in a Trick," a man buys a horse with a bag of pebbles, deceiving the seller. Tao Jang, the judge, has a prisoner marched about in a cangue, and announces that the horse thief has been caught. Then he sets his undercover agents about the city. One of them overhears a man saying how relieved he is. The man is taken in and confesses to his crime.

1.   Nishijin, famous even today for textile making.

2.   Four *kamme* or about thirty-three pounds of gold (avdp.).

3.   *Tanomoshi* fund is a common term for a collection taken up by guild members to assist a friend in need.

4.   Ebisu was one of the Seven Deities of Fortune, usually depicted holding a sea bream and a fishing pole.

5.   Daikoku, also one of the Seven Deities, carries a large bag and a small hammer. He is depicted sitting on two bags filled with rice, and is commonly enshrined with Ebisu. He is called *Makahala* in Sanskrit.

6.   White robes are part of the custom of preparing for death.

7.   One would write that he was innocent on a paper bearing the seal of the Go-ō deity of Kumano. Using this paper as protection for his hand, he would then grasp a red hot bar; if the words on the paper were true, it was supposed to protect the holder from burns. It is called *shimmon-tekka.*

5. THE WONDERFUL POTION THAT CALLS ONE'S NAME

1. Sado Island, a part of present-day Niigata prefecture, located in the Japan Sea, is a former site of rich gold mines in the seventeenth century.

2. Monkey who falls from a tree is one who is without familial aid, because he has left his relatives.

6. TWINS WHO BREAK A BLOOD TIE

1. Generally, mourning observances were held on the seventh day (after death), fourteenth day, twenty-first day, twenty-eighth day, and thirty-fifth day. Sometimes this was followed by the forty-second-, forty-ninth-, and hundredth-day memorial services.

2. The head clerk had the authority and responsibility to look after the welfare of the home.

3. Customarily, the eldest son would inherit the household and family name, while the younger brothers would marry into another family and receive that family's name.

7. NINE DRINKS OF SAKE—AND LIVING

In *Itakura Seiyō,* Book VIII, 6, "On the Case between the Wife and Concubine," the son of a legal wife and the son of a concubine feud over who should be the heir to the estate of their father.

1. Ten-drink *sake* cup. A *sake* cup which would tip when empty or overfilled, but would stand upright when almost (nine-tenths) full.

2. Yen Shih. A master craftsman of the Chou Period (1120–294 B.C.).

8. A GIFT OF A FALSE SLEEVE

1. A man's twenty-fifth or forty-second year was considered to be particularly perilous.

2. Women of ages nineteen and thirty-three were believed to be similarly endangered.

3. *Sumi-maegami* style. The hairstyle of a youth who had not yet taken the adult initiation rites.

Part II
DISTINCTION

1. The Short Bow
of the Ten-night Nembutsu

A long time ago in the Capital, there lived a man from Saga named Anrakubō, who supplemented his income by singing the Hayari Nembutsu.[1] The thin, yet resonant, quality of his voice was unlike that usually heard in sutra chanting; his singing, in fact, inspired his listeners with religious thoughts and made them yearn for the life hereafter.

It was the tenth night of a ten-night mass.[2] The Nembutsu fraternity were in one of their useless assemblies. The beating of chimes by priests and laymen alike reverberated until dawn. All of them sought an invisible paradise.

The next morning, as the shop doors were opening on Matsubara Avenue, the mist of dawn cleared on the Higashiyama hillside and revealed the corpse of a man of forty-two or forty-three, with a Jōdo rosary on his left hand and an arrow in his ribs. Someone recognized the man and identified him: "It is the owner of the pipe store in front of the Great Buddha."[3]

A town councillor was dispatched to notify the wife. She came immediately, in great shock; her grief was not small. "Here last night just after dark, you went to the Nembutsu meeting in the Inaba Yakushi Temple neighborhood,[4] and now what terrible fate has come upon you?"

She turned to her fellow worshippers for assistance. They were all elderly people of spiritual bent, and all aspired to the world hereafter. They were greatly saddened by his untimely death: "To think that all of us relied on him to pray for our souls after we die," they said, and offered candlelight, incense, and flowers. None of them could be suspected of the crime, so the widow took the suit to the magistrate.

After carefully investigating the case, His Lordship inquired: "Is there anyone among his acquaintances you might suspect?"

The wife reflected for a time and said: "There are two people with whom my husband was especially friendly but broke off with four or five years ago." She gave their names.

The men were summoned and interrogated as to the reasons for their estrangement from the dead man. One of them answered: "I was his companion at *kemari*[5]; we strove together at this art and were an even match, but then I was admitted into the Kemari school and eventually permitted to wear the purple waistband. That made him jealous, and he stopped playing ball with me; gradually our meetings became less frequent."

Then the other man testified: "We both competed for the same courtesan, Kagetsu, in the geisha district near Rokujō; but that only lasted for a short time, and gradually our acquaintanceship fell away. Months and years have passed, but the woman is still working there. Summon her, I beg you, to confirm what I have said."

His Lordship decided that these two men had no reason to kill and said: "You two were close friends of the deceased and cannot be indifferent to his sudden end. In memory of your past association, therefore, why don't you give his wife a *kamme* of silver each to help with funeral expenses?"

One man consented, but the other demurred, pleading hardship. "I barely have enough resources for myself," he said, "and this would be a burden to me."

With this the man who had been so willing to contribute was looked upon with suspicion and interrogated. He said: "My wealth is secure; there isn't a person who doesn't know that I make a living by lending money, not only to the people of this district, but also to people all over the capital. Even if I gave a bag of silver as a condolence offering, it would not strain my purse. That's why I consented to your suggestion." The explanations of both men seemed most reasonable, and without further questioning their trial was terminated. The two men returned to their respective homes.

After they left, His Lordship spoke to the widow: "There is no way to investigate this case any further. Resign yourself to the fate which unexpectedly claimed your husband and send the corpse to Toribeno for burial.[6] Your husband's enemy was the arrow; bury it in the urn with his ashes. Since you have no children, you are at liberty to remarry after one hundred days of mourning." Everyone departed respectfully and did as His Lordship suggested. That year passed quickly.

It was the spring following, and just past midnight, when it was still dark and all were asleep, the voice of a woman was heard near Matsubara Avenue where the man had been shot the year before. She knocked loudly on the doors, awakening everyone. "It's a robber! Come out quickly! Come out!" she shouted.

The residents came out in great alarm, each armed with a club. Among them was one determined man holding a bow and arrow. Law officers who lay concealed in the shadow of the houses surrounded the man and bound him. "If you have anything to say, say it at the Magistrate's Office," they said and led him off as his neighbors watched.

"The woman who woke people last night," said His Lordship, "was the wife of the man you slaughtered one night last year. I sent her out last night expressly to carry out a plan I had developed. You responded by coming out with a lethal weapon inappropriate for the occasion. Can you explain why?"

The arrested man said calmly: "This short bow was left me by my parents. I had it near my pillow as usual, and when I was roused by the word 'Robber,' I grabbed it without thinking about it."

"Well, maybe what you say is true, but let us compare this arrow with the arrow of a certain case." The order was given, the urn of the murdered man was dug up, and when the arrows were compared there was not a single difference between them.

"Now what was the grudge that made you kill that man?" asked His Lordship.

The suspect was no longer able to pretend innocence and confessed: "Not too long ago, I took up the sport of archery. I gradually became able to hit my mark, and often shot foxes and cats. When I became skillful, I had the urge to shoot a human being. I had no ill feeling of any kind, but when late one night I was fortunate enough to see someone pass by, I unleashed my arrow."

"You employed a martial weapon inappropriate for a townsman, and, furthermore, you committed manslaughter. You are a criminal; there is none like you in this wide capital," said His Lordship. Then he passed sentence.

The bow and arrow were hung on a high signboard which explained the crime, and the man, it is said, was executed.

2. The Overtones of Kanehira

A long time ago in a town of the Capital, as the story goes, a certain person quickly lost a lawsuit he should have won because he talked too much. In Shiga-no-Ura of Gōshū (present-day Shiga prefecture), there stood a small shrine in the shade of a pine tree. Tradition held it to be a branch shrine of the Mountain King, so from ancient times it was affiliated with Mount Hiei. However, of late worshippers made pilgrimages there even on nonfestive days, and the contribution box became heavy.

Now this is a world where any one can fall prey to avarice. The villagers of Shiga discussed the matter of the shrine and said, "There is no reason why we should allow the priests of Mount Hiei free access to this shrine. It should be treated as part of our village." They decided to hire a lawyer, and soon it became a case for the Magistrate's Office in Kyōto.

"State the reasons that lead you to question the ownership of this shrine which in the past has belonged to Mount Hiei," the villagers were asked.

Their eloquent counsel stepped up and replied: "There is an old poem that refers to 'the lonely pine of Karasaki of Shiga',[1] but I have never heard of one referring to 'the lonely pine of Mount Hiei!' This shrine we have dedicated under the pine tree must be that shrine of Shiga, Karasaki."

His arguments were convincing, but the priests of Mount Hiei countered with another strong old precedent. The discussion went on, whereupon Mr. So and So of Karasaki village stepped up and said: "In the noh play, too, Kanehira sings: 'Oh, the rippling waves by Shiga's Karasaki and its Lonely Pine. . . . ' "

A priest who was a skilled debater stepped up and said: "This man is undoubtedly a master of song. Let us hear, kind, sir, how that beautiful song ends."

His Lordship had perceived what the priests were up to and ordered that a hand drum be brought. "Now, I will play the hand drum, and we shall go on with the court proceedings. Continue with the song," he ordered.

The Karasaki village man could not refuse, and so, in all seriousness, he sang there in the courtyard:

Oh, the rippling waves
By Shiga's Karasaki
And its Lonely Pine—
A branch of the procession
Of the arks of Seven Shrines.[2]
That's what it is.

When the song was over, His Lordship set his drum down and said: "Seven Shrines! Then it is the Mountain King Pine!"

Thus, thanks to this very song, the case was won by the Mount Hiei side. The priests shouted in unison: "What accomplishment! Bravo! Bravo!" After praising His Lordship, they left the court.

3. The Fifty-night Dream of Buddha

A long time ago in the Capital, lived a man who had a strange dream. He was a watchmaker by profession, whom the sound of bells had awakened from his slumbers in the floating world. After that he prayed from dawn to dusk for the world hereafter and was nicknamed Shaka-emon.

His hair was crinkled to match his name, and his appearance was quite striking. For a long time he lived in a rented home below Karasuma. He was a member of the Ikkō sect, but it was no secret that he hated religious observances. When he was in charge of food preparations one November 28th,[1] he held a barbecue.

One day when four or five of his neighbors were gathered together, Shaka-emon the boarder came in, made his obeisances, and said: "I have been dreaming a strange dream night after night; last night was the fiftieth in a row. The message still rings in my ears, and somehow I cannot believe it is only a dream. I am convinced that a nine-inch golden statue of the Buddha, which is probably a creation of Kōbō Daishi,[2] is buried under the bedroom of this home. It radiates golden rays to my pillow and speaks gracious words: 'Thou art one who is close to Buddha. For the sake of future generations, thou must dig it up. It will save many sentient beings and people who are now suffering.' This shows, I am sure, His concern for us all. I will pay the expenses for the carpenters and diggers: please permit me to dig it up today."

The homeowner, who did not believe in the the teachings of Buddha, heard his request, clapped his hands and laughed: "If dreams are so reliable, I would purchase that dream for a thousand pieces of silver and dig it up myself."

In the group was a man of more prudence, who advised: "Now that we have heard this, it is not proper that we do nothing about it. If he is willing to finance the project, he should be given permission." The homeowner finally agreed, and pushing aside all his possessions and furniture, he took up the floor boards. Pick and shovel clanked away till dawn. They dug five yards down, but nothing resembling a Buddha statue appeared. All they found were a chipped tea jar, some burned out charcoal and a discarded top shell.

Enthusiasm waned, and the hole was filled as before. The host said in anger, "I knew from the beginning that things would end up this way." The boarder, at a loss for words, quietly returned home.

The following day, he came back and said to the homeowner: "Last night, I had a clear vision of the Buddha and prayed to him. It is located just two or three *sun* deeper and to the southeast. It is very regrettable that we did not dig just a little more yesterday. It is the Buddha's fervent wish that it be dug up. I beg you to let me do so."

Once again, the digging began, and this time, true to the revelation, the statue of the Buddha appeared. Everyone prayed in gratification. First of all, they washed it off, and the glow of the body was so restrained that it seemed indeed to be an antique Buddha; greed filled the heart of the homeowner. "This image is mine," he claimed.

The boarder remonstrated with him: "I paid all the costs; the Buddha is mine."

"I consented to your request because you pleaded so earnestly, but I never promised that the Buddha would be yours," the other man said. Thus it became a case for His Lordship.

The magistrate first listened to the claims of the two men. Next, he ordered the Buddha sealed in a container and kept for three days. Then he summoned the Buddha image craftsmen of the capital and inquired: "Approximately how many years was this statue buried?" They examined it carefully and replied: "We believe it was in the ground five to seven years."

Next, certain townsmen were summoned, and His Lordship asked them: "How many years has it been since the home was purchased?" The townsmen answered, "It is over forty years." Then Shaka-emon was called in. His Lordship said: "You villain! You attempted to give people the impression that you were praying for the life hereafter, but you were evil at heart. You have plotted this for a long time, and on the day the hole was first dug, you buried the statue. The next day you dug it up, letting the news spread throughout the capital. You plotted this with an accomplice, a renegade priest, and undoubtedly you have had great plans of gathering money from contributions. Confess the truth. If you continue to lie to us, we will resort to various interrogation methods."

Shaka-emon was filled with dismay, opened his heart and told all, explaining that poverty had driven him to evil. "You are a villain, particularly in your use of the Buddha to deceive others. You are the worst of evildoers and should be severely punished. However, since you have not harmed anyone else, your life will be spared," said His Lordship. "As penalty for this crime, you must carry a hoe with that statue tied to the handle, bearing an explanation on a placard through the streets of Kyōto for three days so everyone can see this thief of the world hereafter.[3] After that, you will be expelled from the Capital. As for the homeowner, he caused unnecessary vituperation and is almost as guilty as the other man. For this crime, he shall wear *hakama* and a sleeveless coat,[4] and, carrying a placard, shall accompany Shaka-emon around the Capital." This was their sentence.

4. Bitter Feelings
over Marriage to a Neighbor

Long ago in a town of the Capital, there lived a famous Kanoko weaver named Korin of Omiya.[1] She was as beautiful as the great courtesan of Rokujō, and men loved her desperately for the grace of her movements. She was, however, cold-hearted and purely out of calculation took a blind *rōnin* (unemployed samurai) for a husband. He was, in fact, a samurai of good lineage with wealth enough to last a lifetime who lived in the Capital because he enjoyed the life there. He had an apartment in the suburbs of the East temple,[2] where he had lived without a care until one day he heard rumors as to the beauty of this woman. He then made inquiries as to whether money could win her hand in marriage. Korin consented, and they exchanged vows as man and wife.

For three to five years they lived on their wealth, dining extravagantly and wearing elegant clothes. But the woman's insatiable craving for luxury soon seriously reduced their fortune. Then she became harsh toward her sightless husband, and began to think of getting a divorce. At this time she met a young *rōnin* who lived in the same neighborhood and was an acquaintance of her husband. This man was wealthy, and Korin's affection swayed toward him; in secret, they exchanged lover's vows.

Then she feigned illness and urged her husband to file the divorce papers. She had someone sign for him and freed herself from her husband. Before ten days had passed, she moved in to live with the other man. There were no intermediaries; she cared little about the criticism of society.

Even outsiders could not help feeling resentment toward this woman when they realized what had happened; all the more unbearable was the outrage of her former husband. He contemplated murdering her and committing suicide, but since, after all, he had divorced her, he feared that people would talk about the matter after his death. He therefore thought it better to leave matters as they were.

To add insult to injury, one night a notice was affixed to his gate saying: "If this *rōnin* is allowed to continue living here, he is apt to start running around swinging his sword, and nobody's life will be safe."

The blind *rōnin* commented to his neighbors on the notice: "This is not something I cannot bear. I don't know what grudge anyone might have against me, but if my presence here causes other people anxiety, it might be better if I left."

Everyone sympathized with the *rōnin* and said that the note was without grounds. "Please remain here as if nothing happened," they said, soothing him, but he replied: "I appreciate your kind thoughts from the depths of my heart, but this matter troubles me, and I cannot leave it unsettled. I don't want to trouble the people of this town, so I will take it up with His Lordship."

His Lordship inquired: "Do you have any idea who would want to do such a thing?" The blind man answered: "I don't want to suspect anyone, but until recently I lived with my wife, who suddenly told me that she had become ill and asked for a divorce. Thinking it fate, I carried out her wishes, but nine days later she married a neighbor. I was a good friend of this man before, but since the marriage I have not gone to his dwelling. Other than he, I cannot think of anyone who could be suspected," he said.

After hearing this explanation, His Lordship summoned the husband and wife in question. "Surely you were having an affair. You, lady, are the great villain. As for the man, if you were once a friend of this *rōnin,* simply out of duty to preserve social order you should not have married this woman. No doubt you had illicit relations with her when she was still the wife of the blind *rōnin.* If you don't confess the truth, you will be severely interrogated," His Lordship threatened.

The wife replied, "The truth is that my present husband forced me to file for divorce. That's why things came to this pass."

"You two should be severely chastised, but since all this happened after the divorce papers were filed, your lives will be spared, but the woman's nose shall be cut off and her husband's head will be shaved. Then you shall be expelled from the Capital." Thus the sentence was passed.

After that His Lordship called the *rōnin* before him and commended him: "I believe it was you who hung the notice in order to create grounds for a lawsuit. You did the right thing." It is said that the *rōnin* was struck with admiration at the wisdom of His Lordship.

5. Day Laborers Cost the Capital Money

A long time ago in the Capital, when one gazed from the West Gate of Kiyomizu Temple,[1] one could see private homes stretching out endlessly under growths of dense trees. The white walls of the three-storied storehouses reflected the sunset, and even though no one knows what all may be stored inside them, it is said that "Storehouses are the flowers of the wealthy." Gradually, even the Lower District flourished, and the fields became filled with homes.

At that time, there lived in the seventh ward a rice dealer who did business over a wide area. In recent years, he had become one of the millionaires of the town. He kept the main part of his home unchanged but built several additions until, finally, there was no space left for further building. On the boundary between his property and the next village, he built a two-story fireproof storehouse three *ken* by five *ken* in length. On the windows, screens were fastened, covered by copper shutters; under the eaves, iron gutters were installed; the construction was splendidly finished.

Then a messenger dispatched by a landlord of the next town arrived. "It appears that your storehouse has intruded two *shaku* and five *sun* into our side of the land.² This is an unlawful act," the messenger protested. Shocked, the wealthy man checked the village borderline and discovered that the storehouse had unmistakably encroached to a distance of three *shaku*.³

All the neighbors congregated and after discussion of the matter said: "It is not because this master was too lazy to survey his estates before constructing the storehouse. It has all come from the avarice of his late father." Thus they censured the dead father. Actually, until recently, the area behind this storehouse had been wild fields; the boundary had not been determined, and a hedgerow protruded onto the neighbor's land. The storehouse had been built without surveying the boundary, an oversight of the town government. The neighbors decided to apologize and beg the indulgence of the neighboring villagers.

"When the storehouse next requires repair, I will cut off the overlapping area and rectify the error. If you decide to utilize the land before that time comes, I will surrender it at that time without delay. If you consent to leave the land in cultivation for the time being, I will pay fifty *me* of silver annually,"⁴ said the owner, attempting to appease the neighboring villagers. They were not, however, easily won over.

"He has been poaching on land here for a long time, and now is the time to punish him in front of everyone." Knowing that the storehouse owner was affluent, they made exorbitant demands, thinking to acquire much wealth in the process. The storehouse owner realized that he was in trouble and offered two *kamme* of silver and profuse apologies, but they paid no heed. He found it impossible to resolve the matter. The other parties could not back down after presenting their demands, so they brought the complaint, including maps of the area, before the magistrate.

His Lordship summoned both parties. "One who erects a building so large it encroaches on another's land commits an act of impropriety," His Lordship stated. "He should be chastised, but this man built it by his father's plans without any complicity of his own and he could not have acted if the town councillors were vigilant. Although the overextended building is located in an open area, there is no reason that the town should exempt this house alone from its jurisdiction. This very day, the area should be roped off and the storehouse excised. The prosecution's complaint is entirely correct. No complaints will be heard over the dust from the work. Care should be exercised, however, that neighboring cultivated areas are not harmed.''

Day laborers and carpenters numbering nearly a hundred were hired. Within four hours, all was dismantled, and the roof line made shorter than before. It was indeed a deplorable sight, and everyone reflected as to how sad the storehouse owner must be. The townspeople watching shed tears and felt resentment toward their uncompromising neighbor. Soon His Lordship was informed that the storehouse had been shortened. "Calculate the total amount of money spent in the work," was the order given. The account book was presented: the amount was 874 *mon* 2 *bu* of silver. "The bill should be given to the one who requested that the storehouse be shortened."

That man protested: "This is a burdensome decision." But His Lordship said, "You are a villain who has caused this Capital to incur great expense. In fact, when the foundation walls of the storehouse were being laid, you already knew what the outcome would be. But, even when the wooden walls were being constructed you remained silent. When the roof tiles had been laid and the building was given its final coat of paint, then and only then did you demand its demolition. You are a knave! If you don't have the cash available, sell your home and pay the bill!" was the order.

Having no alternative, the man auctioned off his home for one *kan* two hundred *momme* on that very day.[5] From that amount, 874 *mon* 2 *bu* was allotted to pay for the warehouse cost. Three hundred *mon* was taken by other bill collectors. Finally, with only 7 *mon* 3 *bu*—four pieces of silver—in his wife's rosary bag, he left, it is said, the town in which he had lived for a long time.

6. Bills for Sea Bream, Octopus, and Perch

A long time ago in a town of the Capital, an enterprising fish merchant of Nishiki-no-Tana saw the spring as the bream of cherry blossoms and autumn as the crucian carp of maple leaves.[1] There came a time, however, when he had so much difficulty collecting money owed him that he could no longer support himself. So he made up bills for thirty-eight buyers and entered on them only the amount owed, leaving off the name of the buyer. He then posted them on the wall of the magistrate's mansion.

Officers of the court took down the bills and reported to His Lordship. "If these bills are genuine, the unpaid money should be paid," said His Lordship and stamped them with his seal. They were again posted on the gate pillar, whereupon the fish dealer took them down during the night and returned home. Ten days later, he posted them again with a message attached: "Thanks to Your Lordship, I was able to redeem all of these unpaid bills."

The officers thought the matter strange and waited until His Lordship was in a congenial mood to inquire about it. "The bills were of sales to temples. The temples these days are rank with carnivorous priests," he said with a laugh.

7. Something for the Deaf to Hear

A long time ago in the outskirts of the Capital near Kitano, lived a man who ran a pawn and sake shop. He soon became a millionaire, and as his business prospered he acquired as a servant a seamstress accustomed to wearing very attractive clothing. After a time, she began to crave green plums, and it gradually became apparent that she was pregnant. Her mistress inquired about the matter and exhorted the woman to reveal her lover's identity. But she kept the name a deep secret and would not confess, to the annoyance of her mistress. Deemed unsuitable for continued service in this household, the woman was sent home to her parents.

A half year later, the master suddenly complained of feeling dizzy and collapsed. Everyone tried to rouse him, but his breathing had stopped;

nothing could be done. He had left no child to succeed him; so the grief of the widow was indeed great. Moreover, the birthplace of the widow was in Dewa (present-day Yamagata and Akita prefectures), and she had no relatives in the Capital.

Shortly after the relatives had arrived and gathered to prepare for the burial, the seamstress reappeared, carrying a suckling child in her arms. She said: "The heir to this home is this baby. There is no doubt it was the late master who fathered the child. The incident can be verified by the head servant." Then, ignoring the solemnity of the occasion, she began to wail.

The head servant came forth and said: "What she says goes beyond my wildest dreams."

Then the woman said: "On a certain occasion, you delivered silver from the master for this baby's upbringing."

"What? I don't even know where your parents' home is," he replied.

The woman clung to him and said: "Even though this child is too young to know east from west, he has the master's blood in him. Heaven will punish you for pretending ignorance when you know the truth."

The woman's eyes glistened with tears, and she tearfully approached the dead master. She clutched at him though he was dressed in mourning clothes; his white robe came off, his *eboshi* hat fell to the floor. The shocking event in which a funeral was interrupted became a court case and the details were presented to His Lordship. The head servant was summoned. "Is that child the master's son? State the truth!" said His Lordship.

"This was my master's business; I knew nothing about his personal concerns. I only carried out his orders by going to her parents' home in Fujinomori the first of every month and delivering fifty *me* of silver.[1] Other than that, I know nothing," the servant replied.

"He would not have had you take the money every month without a reason," His Lordship said. "It is now clear why, when the mistress inquired about the matter, the seamstress did not reveal the master's part in it but took all the blame and returned to her parents' home. That child, as son of the deceased man, should become the heir. His mother should remain in the household as his foster mother, and though he is her son, she should rear him as if he were her master. The widow should act as his mother and, if she wishes, go into permanent retirement. The gold and silver will be guarded by the family and neighbors. The earnings on it will be made public yearly. The business will be entrusted to the clerks until the son is fifteen years of age, when he will receive all of it. All matters will be supervised by the widow. If at any time anyone suspected of being the child's father appears, the matter should be reported regardless of the time that occurs. The deceased man shall be buried forthwith."

Thus the sentence was passed. The funeral was carried out with the child acting as the heir.

While the widow mourned the death of her husband, she continued to question the origin of the child of the servant. After all, she and her husband had long bewailed their lack of a child, and by mutual agreement had brought in a number of seductive courtesans, all of which had failed to provide them with the heir they sought. She could not understand why her husband had concealed this new development.

Meanwhile, she pretended to be deaf. She detached herself from worldly matters, devoted herself to services before the family altar, and spent her days inconspicuously. The next year arrived, the time of the vernal equinox, which was also the time for the memorial services for the deceased master. Everyone in the household visited the family temple to present fragrant flowers at the grave and offer prayers, but the widow indulged herself only in memories of the past, as tears fell to dampen her sleeves. She gently took the hand of her adopted son and said: "Your papa has turned into this gravestone. Now pour some water for him."

On hearing the widow utter these words, the real mother was very amused. "His real father is right here wearing the *haori* with vertical stripes. He is healthy and very much alive. You don't know what you are saying, you hopelessly deaf one," she said, looking at the servant, who was the child's real father.

The widow acted as if she had heard nothing and returned home. But early the following morning, she went to His Lordship's mansion and declared: "I don't want a bit of the wealth, but if someone who is of no blood relation succeeds to this home, how grieved my deceased husband will be viewing it from the shades of grass and leaves." Then she explained what she had overheard the day before.

His Lordship summoned the foster mother and the servant in question and interrogated the mother. "What is the reason for saying that this servant is the father of your son? There is a person who is sure she heard this yesterday and has filed a suit. The servant and the woman replied at once: "Your Lordship, where did she hear this? Surely it is a groundless accusation the widow's relatives have dreamed up to discredit us so they can choose an heir from among themselves and have a free hand with the wealth. The mistress has been deprived of her sense of hearing since about April or May of last year. We have given her countless drugs and even presented one thousand dishes to the Inaba Yakushi deity,[2] but all our supplications have been in vain. Since then, all communication has been in writing. This fact is known not only in the household but throughout the town. Please investigate whether the widow heard our conversation imperfectly."

At that moment, the widow broke out laughing. "I did not believe you from the beginning, so I took the pardonable liberty of pretending to be deaf,'' the widow said, as she explained various matters which she had overheard in the past year. The servant and the foster woman turned crimson and were lost for an answer.

After further interrogation, His Lordship found that the servant was undeniably the father of the child, and decided that these two people should be executed. But the widow intervened and requested that the couple be spared in memory of her husband. The servant could not be pardoned, but the maid was sentenced to sit on the Gojō bridge with a large mortar bowl on her head, a bamboo bellows (bamboo tube through which one blows to encourage a fire) in one hand, and a rice scoop in the other. She was to wear clothing that would clearly show her to be a maid-servant and remain there for three days as an example of one who had lied about her master. The child was remanded to the custody of the maid's parents with the understanding that he would eventually become a priest. Thus, the sentence was passed.

8. The Departed Spirit Facing the Mountain of Swords

A long time ago in the Capital, there lived a man who thought only of this world and forgot completely about the world hereafter. His only joy was to accumulate gold and silver. Just when his home began to enjoy prosperity, his greed caused him to use force when collecting from a debtor as short-tempered as he, and in the altercation he stabbed the man to death and then died himself.

Everyone said that his life had been shortened by heaven in requital of his daily actions. They placed his body in the coffin as it was, without washing it, and as the Sembon temple bells sounded thrice,[1] the hapless smoke rose, and they returned home.

The son of the greedy man, in contrast to his late father, set his heart on the path of Buddhahood. After this incident that had separated him from his father, he felt keenly the impermanence of this floating world and set his heart on becoming a priest someday. His mother dressed her hair in widow's style,[2] presented flowers every day, and sank herself in grief.

On the forty-ninth day of mourning,[3] an itinerant priest of about thirty came and inquired about the name of the family. He then quietly entered the home and said something like this: "At Tateyama in Etchū province (modern-day Toyama prefecture that faces the Japan Sea), I was entrusted with something by your husband.'' He then mentioned how the dead man had said to him, ''Take this dagger, and using it as a symbol of me, please pray for my soul. The gold and silver I have accumulated all these years will be an obstacle to me in the world hereafter, so give it all to charity. In my present sad state, I have come to regret my greed of past days. Please help me to come closer to the Buddha.'' On hearing this heartrending report, the mother and son felt as if their souls had left them.

''Let us,'' said the son, ''ask this priest to stay here until we build a chapel, where he can say a 10,000-day mass for the departed. In accordance with his wishes, let us contribute every bit of our gold and silver.'' The mother and son then asked the priest to stay and he replied: ''I shall stay with you gladly, but not until I have made a pilgrimage to Kurodani.''

When the neighbors heard of this incident, they advised: ''The dagger which your husband carried was shown to His Lordship and then placed in the coffin and burned with the corpse. It is uncanny that it should appear here again. We cannot allow this matter to pass without investigation!''

The matter was brought before His Lordship, who heard it and asked: ''After your husband died, was there any man or maid servant or anyone whom you dismissed?''

The widow replied: ''Thirty-five days after the death of my husband, the servants' term came to an end. Taking this opportunity to decrease the number of servants, I dismissed Rokushaku and one waiting-woman. After leaving our service, Rokushaku rented a room in this district. As for the maid, she returned to her parents' home in Shibutani.''

Then His Lordship spoke to the townspeople: ''This priest is probably living with the waiting-woman. Go there immediately and investigate this matter.''

Led by one of the townspeople who knew the way, the officials went to the woman's home and found the priest in question there. He had removed his priestly garments and had just finished frying the head of an Ōmi crucian carp when he and the woman were arrested and taken to His Lordship.

His Lordship said to the woman: ''Soon after the dagger was placed in the casket, you took it out unbeknownst to anyone. Then you became intimate with that priest and knowing well the grief of the mother and son, plotted to reap much gold and silver by this deception. You are a malefactor who has desecrated your late master's name.'' After interrogation, the couple confessed everything much as His Lordship had described it, and, it is said, they were both executed.

9. A Kyōto Wife
with Clear Title
Is Sent Away

A long time ago on Ogawa Avenue in the Capital, there was a shop famous for its wheel-spun yarn. In such a shop, a woman is first of all an ornament, and the proprietor had an eye for gorgeous costumes as well as new mistresses. During his life he had twenty-eight or twenty-nine wives, much to the amusement of his neighbors who counted. Even terrible affairs like this fail to create comment after a time, and the Capital is, after all, very large; therefore in spite of the brides' being thrown out on the street after settling for less than ten days, the brides kept coming in a seemingly endless stream.

This man went on, afflicted with wine and women, recklessly destroying himself without letup. The belongings of one wife would come in on the same night another wife's belongings were being taken out. Finally the marriages were being carried out without even a matchmaker.

Even this, however, came to an end. He was gradually reduced to the state of a myrrha (a living mummy, skin and bones), and then, as if nodding off to sleep, left this world. His bride of that night was a widow by morning.

The deceased left no child, but only a younger brother who was not very bright. The townspeople felt pity toward the younger brother and advised him to marry the widow and succeed to the estate. The widow, however, was one who looked out for her own interests and demurred. She wished to give a small part of the wealth to the younger brother and have him leave the home. She argued: "Out of concern for me, my husband said: 'You were fated to be my last wife, and so I shall leave all to you.'" Since her case depended on the words of a dead man, the case was taken to His Lordship.

The decision was handed down: "Let the younger brother succeed to the home. Give the widow an equal amount of the wealth and have her depart. There is no reason that the widow should have the home." She was an articulate woman and said, "I am now a *goke,* a widow. Everyone knows that the word means, 'the one who succeeds to the home.'"

"What a clever woman you are to go into the etymology of the word! But it appears to me that you, at the height of your youth, will find it difficult to remain a widow. I suggest you keep in mind that the time will come when you will wish to remarry. Most women find the life of the widow hard to take. Come back again after giving the matter your careful consideration,'' he directed.

When the widow returned, she wore a pious expression and robes of a charcoal-color. ''This is regrettable,'' His Lordship said. ''Why this?''

The widow replied, ''I cannot find it in my heart to seek another husband. I have assumed the garments of one praying for the soul of her deceased mate.''

''Very well,'' said His Lordship, ''Since a *shukke*—a convert—is etymologically 'one who has left the home', throw her out.''

NOTES TO PART II

1. THE SHORT BOW OF THE TEN-NIGHT NEMBUTSU

A similar story is in *Itakura Seiyō,* Part VI, 3. In Rokuhara, Kyōto, a night robber kills a man and steals his wealth. The judge of the trial discovers that the wife of the murdered man was an accomplice. In Saikaku's story, the wife is innocent.

1. Hayari Nembutsu, ''Namu Amida Butsu,'' or ''Praise Amida Buddha.'' The Nembutsu with its dance was first created by the Priest Kūya, in the Heian period.

2. Ten-night mass. In the Jōdo sect, extended Nembutsu chanting masses are held from October 6 to 15. This is called Jūya, or Ten Nights.

3. The Great Buddha is located today near Shichijō by Higashiyama. It was built before the Tokugawa Period. The bottom half of the image has been destroyed.

4. Inaba Yakushi Temple is located near Karasuma, Matsubara, Shimogyō Ward in Kyōto. Enshrined there is the Yakushi (Healing) Buddha statue.

5. *Kemari,* a ball-kicking game, was a popular sport of the nobility during the Heian period.

6. Toribeno was located in the Higashiyama mountain range stretching from the area of Kiyomizu temple to Nishi Ōtani mausoleum. It was famous as a place of cremation from the Heian period.

2. THE OVERTONES OF KANEHIRA

In *Itakura Seiyō,* Part VIII, 8, there is a story of a feud between the head Shintō priest of Yagami Daimyōjin of Tamba and the Buddhist priests of that shrine. Professor Teiji Takita has mentioned the similarity of this story with that of Saikaku.

1. An old poem from the noh play ''Kanehira.''

2. The twenty-one shrines of San-ō (Mountain King), or Hie Shrine, were divided into seven main or upper shrines, seven middle shrines, and seven lower shrines.

3. THE FIFTY-NIGHT DREAM OF BUDDHA

1. November 28th is the memorial day of Shinran (1163–1262), founder of the Jōdo Shin sect of Buddhism (at that time called the Ikkō sect).

2. Kōbō Daishi (774–835), founder of the Shingon sect of Buddhism in Japan, was known as Kūkai. His posthumous title is Kōbō Daishi.

3.   Thief of the world hereafter. One who has deceived people by taking money from worshippers.
4.   *Hakama,* a formal dress mainly for men.

4. BITTER FEELINGS OVER MARRIAGE TO A NEIGHBOR

1.   Kanoko, weaving patterns of white dapples, literally, like a deer.
2.   The East Temple was in the Ninth Avenue, Minami Ward. Its formal name is Kyōōgokokuji. It was built in 796 by Kōbō Daishi.

5. DAY LABORERS COST THE CAPITAL MONEY

1.   Kiyomizu Temple was built in 805 by General Sakanoue no Tamuramaro, who defeated the Ezo of Hokkaidō. It belongs to the Hosshō-Shingon sect.
2.   Two *shaku* five *sun* is about thirty inches.
3.   Three *shaku* is about thirty-six inches.
4.   Fifty *me* of silver is about two-fifths pound of silver (avdp.).
5.   One *kan* and two hundred *momme* are about 9.92 pounds of silver (avdp.).

6. BILLS FOR SEA BREAM, OCTOPUS, AND PERCH

1.   Nishiki-no-Tana is the lane between present-day Teramachi-dōri and Omiya-dōri. Many fish wholesale shops were located there.

7. SOMETHING FOR THE DEAF TO HEAR

1.   Fifty *me* of silver is about two-fifths pound of silver (avdp.).
2.   A form of prayer in which one would offer pottery dishes called *kawarage* to a deity.

8. THE DEPARTED SPIRIT FACING THE MOUNTAIN OF SWORDS

1.   Sembon Emma-dō Temple (Kōmyōzan Injōji is the formal name) is located at the western foot of Mount Funako.
2.   She cut her hair short, which was the custom for widows.
3.   Forty-ninth day of mourning. (See notes, Part I: case no. 6, note 1.)
4.   Servants' term. By custom, in spring, the term was changed on March 5; in autumn it was on September 10.

Part III
THOUGHT

1. Gowns through which Evil Deeds Show

Long ago in the towns of the Capital, if a man of light purse had an attractive daughter, he brought her up in the finest possible style, and, when her charms blossomed, would send her to a *daimyō* (provincial lord) to serve as a lady-in-waiting, or to a high-ranking noble to serve him.

A certain needle-shop owner of Anega Kōji had a daughter of unrivalled beauty. She was sent to serve a great man, to whom she meant more than the moon or the flowers. She was named "Nightingale" by her master, to whom even the New Year's dawn now paled in significance. Deaf to the criticism of society, he ordered that she be addressed as, "Milady." A woman without a name, after all, is just something to ride. (A woman's position is determined by the man she marries.) After that, it became difficult to catch so much as a glimpse of her.

One day, after the dishes for dinner had been set and the maids had noisily left the halls, the lady ate her supper more cheerfully than usual. Shortly afterward, however, she began to suffer sharp chest pains. The color of her eyes faded; her entire body turned purple. Her hands and feet shriveled, her breathing became fainter; she was so ill that she was not able to drink so much as a drop of water. The life of a mortal is frail as the dew; her body withered like a morning glory. "Oh no!" everyone cried in grief.

The maids were distraught and described everything to the physician. He said, "It must have been the combination of the dishes. What did she have for dinner?" She was given medicine to relieve her but to no avail. She suffered for four hours longer and then left this floating world. The master's grief was not small.

After the corpse was taken care of, the physician examined the food. There had been the usual boiled rice. The soup was boiled perch. With the marinated catfish, there was the salmon roe. The fried dish was sea bream salted overnight. With the kneaded bean paste were fish cake rings. There were also *ukogi* broth and fragrant *tōza* pickles.[2] There were no dishes that in combination would be fatal. As he went over various of the suspect foods, the physician noticed that the *miso* had a light greenish tinge. Some was given to the household cat, which a few minutes later appeared to go mad and then fell dead with all four paws curled up.

"There must have been poison in the *miso*," the master thought, and questioned the kitchen help, in particular the maids, but found nothing to implicate one more than another. Then he decided to call in specialists to solve the matter.

The welfare of the maids was important. They could not be treated harshly. It was of particular importance that the guiltless not be made to suffer. "Here is a plan," said the chief investigator, that will cause no more pain than necessary to expose the guilty party."

Immediately, long-sleeved silk kimonos were made for all the sixteen maids. They all put them on and then were housed in the same room. "The guilty person is among you; tomorrow, everyone of you will be tortured," they were told. The lights were turned out and the room was locked from the outside.

It was a summer night, alive with the sound of mosquitoes coming through the bamboo shutters. The maids suffered terribly as their bodies were stung; none had so much as a fan to keep the insects off. They wept in anguish. Some bewailed it as fate. Some chanted, "Nammyō-hōrenge kyō," or other passages from the Kannon sutra. Some talked about their homes and wept. Others sang songs as if nothing had happened. Others made believe they were monsters and went about frightening people. Others indeed bore it all with fortitude. Surely, there is nothing so varied as the heart of man.

Night soon turned into morning and the interrogating officers returned. First, Yanagi, the head of the maids, was questioned. Then the others were called, according to age. Amid all the swoons and the sleep-tangled hair was one maid whose long-sleeved kimono showed not a wrinkle.

"She is the one," an officer said, and had her seized. She was severely interrogated and, with all the shallowness of a woman's heart, confessed. She had acted on the behest of one of the master's earlier mistresses who had been moved by some unknown impulse. The details of the murder were set forth and the guilty parties graciously met their ends.

Afterward His Lordship inquired how the woman's crime was discovered, and he was told: "Those who were innocent were able to sleep in relative ease, and their *kimono*s naturally became untidy. The guilty maid was so concerned about herself throughout the night that she could not rest. Since she did not lie down at all, her *kimono* was by far the least wrinkled. That was the clue by which her guilt was determined."

2. A Note Disappears but Honesty Stands

Long ago in the Capital, there was a wholesaler who dealt in products from the North and lived comfortably in Rokkaku. He had loaned five hundred *kamme* of silver to a friend of his parents, for which he received a promissory note. After payments on the loan had been made for eight years, he sent an emissary requesting payment in order to meet New Year's expenses. The creditor said: "Please bring me the note, and I will pay you the money." When the lender opened the box which contained the note, he found, to his amazement, only a blank piece of paper. He examined the securities filed with it but found these perfectly in order.

The lender discreetly inquired of the borrower how he should proceed. That man said: "I rather believe I paid that money, and since you don't have the note I don't see how you can dispute it." As time passed by his protests about having paid the note became more assured.

Before long the lender found himself the object of slanderous rumors. His very reputation was in jeopardy. It became more than he could bear. He was less concerned about getting the money returned than with reestablishing his good name in the community. He therefore filed a brief stating his side of the matter.

The two parties were called before the court, which proceeded first to inquire of the neighbors about the personal affairs of the disputants.

"The lender," it was said, "has a fortune of at least eight hundred *kamme,* of that we are certain. The borrower, however, has only about thirty *kamme.*" This was the testimony placed before the court.

"The money must still be unpaid," said His Lordship. "Even though the note is now blank it should be paid back. You have attempted a terrible thing and deserve to be punished by society, but if you make restitution no charge will be made against you."

The borrower had no reply save to say: "I shall pay the money as you order."

Then the lender was called up and asked: "Was the note prepared by him and sent to you?"

"Yes," was the answer. "As you point out, it came from him. As I remember the stamp was in perfect order, and it was received and filed."

"From now on, exercise care in your business to have notes executed in your presence. Even in the Capital we have unscrupulous men like this. The note was specially prepared. According to the *Honsō,*[1] something drafted with paste mixed with black squid ink will turn blank after three years. This is certainly what we have here," he said, as the story goes.

3. A Well for
the Life Hereafter

A long time ago in the Capital, there was in the west of Ichijō Avenue a lonely and sparsely populated area. Here lived a poverty stricken old couple who had no children and little hope for the future. Even when they had reached the age when death might claim them any day, they still went to Fushimi daily and bought all the bamboo brooms they could afford; these they sold about the Capital and eked out a living. Gradually, however, their legs began to fail, and they began to worry how they would get about; but fortunately, the world has a way of relieving our worries.

Behind the couple's dwelling, there was a well which had been filled up for many years. If one looked into it, one would find it densely covered with ferns known as *iwahiba*.[1] Rock garden enthusiasts who found it pulled away the moss and in so doing gradually excavated the dirt which had accumulated over the years. Then, suddenly one day, a spring flowed forth. The water was pure and cool. "This is what you must have to relieve the heat of summer," people said and came here to this "Grandfather Spring" from all over the Capital. Soon the old couple lived in ease on their earnings from the water.

Their neighbor on the west observed this and dug to interrupt the water course. As the pure water flowed from his well, the old couple's well went dry. Their income stopped with it. They spent their days grieving about it, helplessly detesting the neighbor more and more as the days went by, becoming carried away with fury as the neighbor began to make money from the sale of water. They then arrived at the terrible resolve of denying the water to everyone. The old man donned a devil mask, put a bear skin over his head, and moved about dimly visible in the nearby bamboo grove to frighten people who came to draw water in the early morning hours. Those who witnessed the sight spread the news, and buyers of water stopped coming.

The neighbor thought this odd: it must indeed be the work of a fox or a badger. He talked it over with his relatives, and they concealed themselves in the undergrowth and observed the scene. The apparition appeared, and they dashed out and beat the thing to death.

They thought they had done a heroic deed, but when they looked at their prey in the dawning, they discovered that it was the old man—their neighbor. They regretted their action, but it was irretrievable. The wife cried in grief, "I want vengeance," and filed suit.

His Lordship listened to her plea and said, "Dressing in such an out of the ordinary way and invading another man's property in the middle of the night was entirely misconceived, and he paid for it with his life. The neighbor, on the other hand, is a greedy man unable to accept the dictates of society. He is a thief who took away the old man's livelihood and stole from him without invading his property. Since he killed the old man for his water, he must erect a grave for him on his property, and he must deflect the water back to its original well in memory of the departed.''

The deceased was buried as ordered, and soon afterward, it is said, the well went dry.

4. A Loser, A Finder

Long ago, an old man was walking on the outskirts of the Capital along the banks of the Kamo River on his way to the Kitayama area where he lived. It was the evening of December 28, and everyone was busy with preparations for the New Year; the old man was returning from a temple service.

In the grass on the edge of the road, he perceived a small package, which he picked up. Inscribed on it were the words: 'three *ryō* in *koban.*' "I don't know who dropped this," he thought, "but he must have been planning to use it for the New Year." He looked down the road in both directions and saw no one. Far off, in the shade of some pines, a person who appeared to be a woodseller had stopped to rest.

The old man approached him and said: "Didn't you drop this?"

"I dropped it," the other man said, "but you have it now, so it's yours."

"That's a troublesome statement to make in these days. Even if I could not find the owner I would not take it home with me. How can I take it when I know who the owner is?"

He then gave the other man the money; he insisted on returning it to the finder. The altercation went on for some time without resolution, with one man throwing it to the other, and the other throwing it back. A seller of cured wood and a herdsman came along and said,[1] in admiration: "This is something rare in these times."

Each of the disputants explained his side of the matter, but the ownership of the coins remained unresolved. It seemed to be something which could only be resolved by a higher authority, so they went to His Lordship and told him what had happened. The officers on duty heard the details and said: "There has never been a case like this. These men are worthy of being called 'Saints of the Capital in Our Time.' ''

When the case was presented, His Lordship was in poor health and involved in consultation with various physicians of the Capital. He therefore asked the Elder Councillor to serve for him. "Take up this matter and show us how wise you are," he said.

This man took up the proceedings with great seriousness and ordered that the three *ryō* of gold coins be produced. To these he added three more coins of his own. Then he took the six *ryō* and separated them into three stacks. "First," he said, to the person who dropped the money, "here are the two *ryō;* you have lost one *ryō*. Now, if the person who found the money takes two *ryō,* he will also have lost one *ryō*. I also stand to lose one *ryō*. Now you will take your money and depart," he ordered.

Everyone commended the Councillor and praised his decision for its wisdom, but when his Lordship heard of it he did not concur: "Your conclusion is incorrect. After all, the man who found the money didn't have to argue with the owner; there were many ways he could have disposed of it. Bringing the matter into court makes it particularly suspicious. The two men undoubtedly want to give everyone in the Capital the impression they are honest so they can cheat everyone later. Call them back!"

The two men were summoned back into court and His Lordship's accusation was repeated to them. "If you don't confess the truth, you will be tortured," they were told, under severe interrogation. The woodseller broke down and confessed: "The other man came to me and asked me to take part, and without reflecting on the consequences, I did as he instructed and posed as the loser."

"Then," His Lordship said, "this evil scheme was plotted by the one who 'found' the money. What I see before me is an aged man who should be walking with a cane. Such misplaced energy! You deserve to be executed, but no one has been harmed by what you have done. So I order you banished from the Capital." Thus the sentence was passed.

As for his accomplice, it is said that he was evicted from the mountain home he had occupied for a long time in the foothills of Mount Kurama.

5. Nembutsus Sold; Metals Chime[1]

Long ago, in the Capital, there was a town populated entirely by worshippers of one religious sect. Throughout the town the Hokke nameplates shone unchallenged. From dawn to dusk, the name of the Lotus Sutra struck the ear. There was, however, one home occupied by a man who followed the Jōdo sect. He would strike his bell and recite the Nembutsu to the annoyance of the Hokke brotherhood.

They came to him preaching the merits of their way, but the man would not be moved. Feeling against this lone nonconformist ran high in all hearts; but he was a homeowner, and they were powerless to act. If he were a renter, he could have been evicted easily; but as matters stood his neighbors could not move against him and they chafed at the restraints that held them.

They consulted with each other and decided: "The man is poor, so let us pay him to change his sect." When they quietly broached the matter to him, he in his greed consented. The entire congregation was delighted and amassed thirty pieces of silver and gave it to the man, who broke with his old faith and joined them.

It was now July 13, and the festivities opened with the Hokke sect bon dance.[2] A mountain of people gathered in front of the convert's gate. On subsequent holy days, and particularly on the day of the memorial services for Nichiren,[3] joyful devotion was accorded by all to both man and wife. But then, when spring and the vernal equinox came in, he returned to his Nembutsu and his bell. The townspeople were shocked and ran to the offender's home: "What is this?" they exclaimed.

The man made a sour face and said: "I've had all of the Lotus Sutra I can stand. I'm saying the Nembutsu and worshipping Amida again."

"What an unscrupulous thing to do! If you feel that way, give us back the money we gave you," they said.

"I don't see why I should return it. You said that if I took up the Hokke faith, my wealth would increase, so I agreed and became a member. But then I got sick of it and am praying once more for the Pure Land. I signed no statement committing myself till my dying day. I am free to follow my own heart," he said, breaking into a strident Nembutsu.

"How awful!" the townspeople said, and filed a suit with His Lordship.

The magistrate called both parties in and heard their claims. He expressed his opinion that the matter had sprung from unnecessary zeal in proselytization to the Hokke sect. Then he went on to say: "The money must be returned and duly received. But here you have taken into the Hokke sect a man who has followed the Jōdo sect since the time of his parents. He must surely have neglected his devotions during the time he followed the Lotus Sutra. I order him, therefore, to compute the number of Nembutsus he has failed to say and have his townspeople say them for him. After that they may accept payment."

Thus the verdict was handed down and the principals sent home. After some discussion among themselves, however, the townspeople decided that reciting the Nembutsu would be burdensome, considered their money lost, and gave up the suit.

6. Wait and the Sums Will Match

Long ago in a town of the Capital, there was a person called "Nodding Granny," who was skilled in arranging marriages. She worked at it throughout the year and never failed at making a match she set her mind to.

Now, there was a man of thirty-five who lied about his age and sought the hand of a maiden of fifteen. After the betrothal gifts were exchanged and all arrangements completed, the parents of the daughter heard that the bridegroom-to-be was older than claimed.

"We have no complaint about his means," they said, "but there is twenty years difference between our daughter's age and his. We cannot give her to him."

The prospective groom, however, demanded that the agreement be fulfilled. The matchmaker had no recourse but to file suit.

Both parties were summoned into court. "If some grave misdeed has been committed by the man, speak out. But if his age is the only problem, you have already accepted the wedding gifts and must now give your daughter in marriage," said His Lordship.

The parents of the girl said: "We were deceived by the matchmaker into making these arrangements. Our daughter is fifteen; the man is thirty-five. There is a difference of twenty years between them. If she were even half his age we would go ahead with the ceremony. We hope Your Lordship will see how we feel about this. It is a poor match; we would like to have the dowry returned."

Then His Lordship said: "If that is what you wish, so be it. Wait five years and then give your daughter in marriage. The man must wait until then. He will be forty; she will be twenty—half his age." This was the order.

7. "Spend the Money" Makes an Unusual Will

Long ago in a town of the Capital called Koromo-no-tana, lived a prudent merchant. People said he was rich, and they were right. He lived a good life, though his body was racked by a disease which weakened him year by year. Finally he saw that death was inevitable and made his will.

He had no children save a son, then in his fifteenth year. The child's mother had died nine years earlier. A second wife had borne no offspring. Even though she was the child's stepmother, she looked at the young heir with affection, showed him every consideration, and in fact, treated him as she would if he were her own child.

The father was satisfied; he could ask nothing more of this world. He bequeathed two hundred *kamme* of silver to his son,[1] twenty *kamme* of silver to his widow to live on,[2] and ten *kamme* to each of his servants, treated equally. It was his wish that the family be managed as before.

He willed keepsakes even to his distant relatives, made a contribution to his family temple, and assigned everything he had. Then he expressed the desire that his fortune be distributed while he was still alive and quickly wound up his affairs.

As the time for his passing approached, he gathered his family and servants together and said: "I feel that this is my last day. I have only one thing left to say. My son will be fifteen years old this year. For the next ten years, until he is twenty-five, you must not restrain him. Don't inhibit him, especially in his love affairs. Even if he spends money as if he is casting it away, let him do as he pleases. But after he becomes twenty-five, if he spends as much as one *sen* foolishly, report it to His Lordship and have him turned out of the house. That is all I have to say." With these words he passed away.

A will saying "Spend the money" did not exist in former ages, and the people of the Capital found it a matter for much discussion and laughter. "He was a shrewd man," they said, "but what can one make of this he did before he died?" The young men of our time are hard to hold down even when supervised.

From the time he was eighteen, the boy began to dip into his fortune.

Those around him had difficulty exercising any restraint on him, and when they gave any indication of attempting that he would say: "You know what my father directed." Thus, deaf to criticism, he lived a life of prodigality. In six or seven years, he had used up one hundred seventy *kamme* of the two hundred *kamme* willed to him.

Everyone was at a loss as to what to do, and he was privately warned often, but he would not listen. The two servants did not know how to proceed, and fearing that his fortune could not last, they petitioned His Lordship. "We humbly beg that this young man be stopped from spending," they pleaded.

His Lordship listened carefully and replied: "According to his father's will, he may continue to spend freely of his fortune for another two or three years. Let him spend his money as he pleases."

One of the servants said, sadly: "But before long the family will be ruined!"

His Lordship answered: "The business will stand. You servants should endeavor to expand it without worrying about his spending. If he fails to act in accordance with his father's wishes after turning twenty-five, then come to me again, and he will be turned out. Most important of all, see to it that he observes due filial piety to his mother."

The two servants did not seem to be satisfied with the words of His Lordship, and perceiving this he said: "You men don't seem to follow me. Your former master, who had such a great reputation here, would not have done an imprudent thing. Return to your duties, and forthwith examine the contents of your storehouses with family members and town officials in attendance."

Accordingly, the two servants returned home and examined the various storehouses and discovered, in a corner where nobody had noticed it, an old chest. On the lid were the words: "This is my image as a golden Buddha. At the time of my thirteenth memorial service open it and give a mass on my behalf."

The lock was broken open, and inside was another box, which contained ten thousand *ryō* of well-wrapped gold coins. This was duly attested to, after which the servants reported what they had found to His Lordship. His conclusion was: "Take care to leave this just as it is. When the son is twenty-five, turn it over to him."

Everyone expressed admiration at the accuracy of His Lordship's conjecture. Some time afterward, the son received the fortune, but because His Lordship knew everything the son was not able to squander a single coin after he was twenty-five, and the house remained solvent.

8. Vase Dug Up,
   A Vessel for Greed

Long ago on the edge of a town of the Capital called Nishi-no-tōin, there was a house with eighteen feet of frontage for sale. A textile painter who had rented in the same town for some time wanted to buy the house but found it more than one man could afford. He therefore went to another man in the same trade, and the two of them bought the house, each taking nine feet.

They moved in and distributed their furnishings but felt somewhat cramped. The location of the well they found particularly inconvenient, and they decided to relocate it at the line that separated the two halves of the dwelling.

Having chosen the area, they now investigated the water course. One night they spread cormorant's feathers, believing that the place where the feathers grew dampest with morning dew would without fail be the spot above clear water. Having determined that spot by ancient precedent, they began to dig.

When the hole had been dug to a depth of about four feet the blades of the digging implements struck something. They looked to see what it was and found a vase sealed with plaster. It bore a wooden tag bearing a date they could not determine precisely. All they could tell was that it had been buried on October 2 in a year of the dragon.

The well digger was delighted. "Look, I've dug up some gold," he said. "Let's have a celebration. That's the way they did it in the old days." (He had been saying self-assertive things like this even before he had dug it up.)

One of the men who owned the home looked in and said: "The vase is on my side, so I'll take it."

The other owner said: "I'm the one who first went about buying this house, so it's mine."

The argument went on endlessly. Word got around among the neighbors that gold had been dug up, and a crowd gathered. The officials of the town conferred and decided that it was a matter that went beyond their authority, so they had a sketch made of the details, placed a number of guards at the well site, and referred the matter to His Lordship.

They explained the matter to him, and he quickly took it up. "Wasn't the man who sold the house and moved away interested in the tea ceremony?" he asked.

An old man came forward and said: "As Your Lordship says, he was indeed devoted to the tea ceremony. But he died fourteen years ago leav-

ing the house to a grandson. It is he who sold it and moved away to the
eastern part of the country."

"The vase can't be very valuable then. The former owner buried it
either to age a new piece or to make it less oily. I award it to both of you:
dig it up carefully, and then use it to keep your greed in," His Lordship
said.

Everyone went back; the vase was opened; lo, there was nothing in it.

9. Warbler on the Branch
   Makes a Wife Cry

Long ago in a town of the Capital, on Sembon Avenue, lived a *rōnin* of
good lineage. He was expert not only at the martial arts but also at
music, and thus was able to mix with men of nobility and live on their
favors.

One evening the first noh recitations of the year were being held at the
home of a person of one of the highest ranks, and the *rōnin* lodged there
for the night. As he looked over the plum hedge of the great library in the
dawning light, he saw that the cherry blossoms had started to bloom with
unusual splendor. The warblers were singing too, and among them was
one that gave forth in the clearest tones the three rays of song.[1] It
perched in the high branches of a willow tree and remained there for
days, giving no signs of departing.

Then the master of the house expressed the desire to have the bird as a
pet. "Fortunately," said the *rōnin*, I know an expert bird catcher; he
lives in Nishi-no-Kyō." The master directed him to get the man.

The *rōnin* went to the bird catcher's home and accompanied him back
to the mansion. The man quickly plucked the bird from its high perch
and captured it. He was given many gifts for his dexterity; then he left
for his home.

The next day the *rōnin* went to the bird catcher's home to congratulate
him on his achievement of the day before. The wife threw herself upon
him in tears, saying: "Where did you take my husband? Why didn't you
let him come home?"

The *rōnin* was at a loss to explain what had happened. "Surely he
returned late yesterday afternoon," he said.

The wife would not listen to his denials. "If you don't know where my
husband is, nobody does. Please send him home," she wailed.

A crowd of neighbors gathered and immediately suspected the *rōnin*.
"Surely you left with him," they said; "and since he hasn't returned,

naturally his wife expects you to explain." Their accusations were reasonable, and the *rōnin* was at a loss to reason them away.

He felt compelled to reveal to her that her husband and he had gone to the Palace the day before, but the wife was not mollified in the least and went forthwith to His Lordship.

The *rōnin* was sent for and interrogated. Then he was asked: "Where did you go with the man yesterday?"

The urgency of the matter was such that he felt bound by the samurai code. "We spent the day talking at my home," he said. For no good reason, he even refused to divulge the name of the man he acted for.

"What house was it that you mentioned to these townspeople earlier?" he was asked.

"I didn't say anything of the kind," he answered.

The *rōnin*'s actions were suspicious indeed. "You are acting in a very guilty manner. If you don't confess, we will torture you and make you speak," His Lordship said.

The *rōnin*'s eyes darkened as he said: "I have no alternative. I killed him."

The wife was beside herself. "Oh, how terrible! Here you were always so friendly with him! Was there a grudge? Did you do it out of greed? You detestable *rōnin*!" she screamed.

His Lordship quieted the woman. Then he turned to the *rōnin*. "Where is the body?" he asked.

The *rōnin* answered without emotion: "I don't know."

"Then why did you say you killed him?"

"If I had not said so, you would have tortured me, and for a samurai to be tortured would be mortifying down to future generations," he said.

His Lordship had begun to believe the man had not committed the crime, so he turned his case over to the officials of his own town. They went so far as to give him back his long and short swords and sent him back.

His Lordship then ordered: "Find out where the bird catcher is. After that has been done, come back again." With that all dispersed.

They searched and found him: "His body was on Takeda Highway, where we didn't expect to find him, murdered."

"It must have been the work of highwaymen. Take care of the body quickly," said His Lordship. "And as for his wife, you have lived with him for a long time and must be suffering greatly. Yet we have no way of investigating further. So get a grip on yourself, and pray for your husband. Since you have no children I know it must be that much harder. And you neighbors of hers, look after her and keep her from need."

On hearing His Lordship's compassionate words, the lady and those with her shed tears of gratitude. "And incidentally, the day after tomorrow, the 19th, is the memorial observance of the death of a close friend of mine, so I would like to make a small offering in memory of this man here. Send someone of the widow's family or some close friend of hers to my door for it," said His Lordship. Then everyone went home, greatly impressed.

Early on the morning of the 19th, a man of twenty-four or twenty-five came to receive the money. His arrival was announced to His Lordship, who asked that the man be shown in.

"How are you related to the widow?" His Lordship asked.

"I'm just a good friend of her husband, so she asked me to come," the man said.

"Wretch!" His Lordship said. "If that's how good a friend you are, today's errand must be for love of it."

The man was interrogated. He was found to be a lover of the woman, who had joined with her in a compact to stab her husband to death. Theirs was a terrible deed, and, it is said, they were executed.

NOTES TO PART III

1. GOWNS THROUGH WHICH EVIL DEEDS SHOW

1.   Ladies-in-waiting or concubines of *daimyō*s (provincial lords) were called *kunijōrō*.

2.   Ugoki broth is made from young leaves and buds of this bush. The scientific name of the plant is *Acanthopanax Sieboldianus*.

2. A NOTE DISAPPEARS BUT HONESTY STANDS

1.   *Honsō Kōmoku*, literally, *"Outline of Plants of Japan,"* 44 volumes.

3. A WELL FOR THE LIFE HEREAFTER

Professor Teiji Takita points out that this story is related to the *kyōgen, Uo shimizu.*

1.   *Iwahiba,* or *Selaginella,* a type of fern.

4. A LOSER, A FINDER

Professor Teiji Takita points out that this story is from *Itakura seiyō,* VII, 14, "Litigation on Holy Men."

1.   Sellers of cured wood were from Yase and Ohara in Rakuhoku, Kyōto.

5. NEMBUTSUS SOLD; METALS CHIME

In *Itakura seiyō,* VI, 6, "Litigation on the Inn Fee," there can be seen the same spirit of the law (court) although the story is different.

1.   Metals Chime is a pun on the chiming of silver coins and the Buddhist altar bell in the home.

2.   Hokke sect bon dance. Believers of the Hokke sect would dance in a circle with fans while reciting the *Nammyō-hōrengekyō* chant for the festival of the dead.

3.   Services were held on October 10.

6. WAIT AND SUMS WILL MATCH

In *T'ang Ying Pi Shih,* 5, "Ch'eng Hao Investigates an Old Man," the problem of age difference is solved in the same way. In *Itakura seiyō,* VII, 13, "Litigation by a Mother and Daughter," the Shoshidai asks the concerned people to wait five years, when they will be forty and twenty; thus the bride will be half the age of the groom.

7. "SPEND THE MONEY" MAKES AN UNUSUAL WILL

1.   200 *kamme,* or 751.9 kilograms (1,654 pounds, avdp. of silver).
2.   20 *kamme,* or 7.52 kilograms (16.54 pounds, avdp., of silver).

8. VASE DUG UP, A VESSEL OF GREED

In *T'ang Ying Pi Shih,* 71, "Ch'eng Pu Investigates the Old Coins": When money was uncovered in the ground of a home, the landlord claimed that it was his father (now deceased) who had buried it. However, when the judge examined the coins, he found that they were minted many years before the time of the landlord's father. So the judge decided that the money did not belong to the landlord.

Part IV
COMPASSION

1. A Wise Woman's Fib

Long ago in a town of the Capital, in front of the Seiganji Temple, stood a large rosary shop run by a man with a wife of stunning natural beauty. Her reputation spread throughout the Capital, and even men accustomed to pulchritude came again and again to gaze on her face. Men from the country were even more attracted by what they heard of her, and when they came to Kyōto they were guided by the owners of the inns where they stayed first to Gion (Yasaka Shrine; gay quarters), then to Kiyomizu Temple, and then to see this wife. Such was her beauty. And so the shop was constantly visited by priests and laity alike, built its business without any outside assistance, and steadily advanced to affluence.

When it seemed that no one in the world was so fortunate as they, the husband suddenly died, leaving his wife a widow at age twenty-five.

She looked as she had before,[1] but her heart had changed. She prayed for the world to come, and lived a life of restraint that surpassed all expectations. All her attention was directed to her son, who had been given his three-year tonsure that year.[2] She had no other wish than to abide his coming of age.

Proposals from suitors and marriage brokers came from all directions, but she turned aside all tenders. The business was, after all, one that a mere woman could run, and it went on just as it had been when her husband was alive. In fact, its profits increased. And yet she lived with no other purpose than to save for her son.

In the neighborhood, in a small rented house, lived a *rōnin* who was a native of Suruga. He was clever at everything, the jewel of the place. People came to him for advice and in return looked after him, installing him as their teacher of noh recitation. Thus he got on for years on a small salary which permitted him to hire a manservant, and thus he learned the ways of the townsmen and gained acceptance among them. Nothing was kept from him; he had the run of their houses.

He had been on particularly good terms with the deceased owner of the rosary shop. Because he wrote with a good hand he was called there twice a year to record transactions.[3] After the proprietor's death he continued to visit when the accounts were rendered.

On the seventh of July he remained there working on the accounts with the young clerks until the stars came up.[4] They had finished recording in the ledger for the festival of the dead all the good fortune it had brought.[5] Sake was brought in as part of the festive mood. He drank more than usual and the conversation quickened. The widow laughed as she seldom did now, and she teased the *rōnin:* "Here a fine man-star like you doesn't even have one rendezvous a year. You are worse off than the Weaver lady!" Then she laughed again.

Until this moment the *rōnin* had led a life of principle, but with this one bit of idle conversation his heart was suddenly wrung. When he left the house he acted as if he was on his way home but instead concealed himself as he passed out the gate and then slipped back under the house. When all was quiet inside, he slipped into the dwelling and stealthily moved back into the inner rooms.

As he approached the widow's bedroom he caught sight of her face through the mosquito netting. This was the woman of such great fame! Her face was even more beautiful than in the daytime. His yearning for her grew even greater.

Her pillow was raised a little; her waistband was untied. Close to her hand lay a short sword. She was the figure of caution, of one who would not be caught unawares even in her dreams. The *rōnin* even feared her, but having come so far he felt he might as well come closer.

The widow started and sat up, yet she did not scream. "What in the world are you sneaking around here for?" she asked the *rōnin.* "If anyone hears you there will be trouble. You had better leave while it is still safe to do so."

Said the resolute *rōnin:* "I have set out to do this; I know I am taking my life into my hands."

The widow was prepared to commit suicide if necessary. "Don't do something you will regret," she said, taking up the dagger and moving onto her knees. She refused all his tenders.

Then she reasoned with him, using every argument she could think of, but he would not listen. Their discussion grew heated, awaking the servants. "Who is there?" they shouted, rising from their beds. The *rōnin* extinguished the lamp and tried to flee, but they surrounded and captured him.

"What a terrible thing!" they said. "Here we thought so highly of him and called him in to help us every year, and now he sneaks up in the middle of the night knowing where all the money is in the mistress' bedroom. Regardless of what our master says, the servants of this house cannot carry out their responsibilities if we let this go unnoticed. We cannot forgive him." Turning aside all moderating words, they brought the matter before His Lordship.

All concerned were called in. His Lordship asked them to state their cases. The *rōnin* said, without raising his voice in the slightest degree and with great eloquence: "What happened is that after the master of this house died, I, who had no wife or children, entered into a secret relationship with his widow. Then she, it seems, found another man and schemed up a way to get me, her lover, into trouble. How shallow is a woman's heart. If she had only said to me, 'Let us end this affair,' and finished it that way! But to get together with the servants and to brand me a thief, how hateful that is. How terrible this woman!"

The widow was furious. "You are a man who makes something out of nothing. I am not such a woman," she said.

They went on exchanging unsubstantiated charges. It seemed as if the dispute would never end, when the widow broke into tears: "I am embarrassed to say it, but there is a reason that I would not be guilty of such behavior. Since I was young I have had a venereal disease. After I was married two or three years, the pain of it prevented my husband and me from having normal marital relations. It was a family matter, and my husband out of consideration for me kept it secret. As the months and years of our difficult relationship passed by, my husband died, and with that I turned resolutely away from concerns with this floating world. That this most recent misfortune has forced me to reveal my affliction surely must stem from uncommom karma." With this she resumed her weeping.

Then the *rōnin* came forward and said: "The woman told me about the illness she mentions, and I took steps to have it cured last winter."

The widow burst out laughing: "I don't have any such illness. Like any normal human being, I have a small mole on my left shoulder, but other than that I don't have the slightest defect. I beg Your Lordship to investigate this matter."

The *rōnin* turned red in the face; he did not say another word.

"So he is the culprit," said His Lordship. "Yet he is not a thief. His misdeed came from his love for a woman without a husband, and so his life will be spared. He will be exiled to his home in Suruga. As penalty for his slanderous assertions, however, half his head will be shaved, and he will be cast out. As for the woman, how admirable is the intelligence she showed at short notice!" Thus, it is said, he commended her.

2. Two Choices:
One Good, One Bad

Long ago in a town of the Capital, many children gathered together and made a festival float imitating those of the Gion Festival.[1] Even the wide avenues seemed narrow as this float creaked through the streets. There were no guardians to accompany the children who carried knives with them. It was indeed a dangerous thing. In the commotion, a boy of seven plunged a large dagger into the mouth of a nine year old and killed him.

The grief of the parents whose son was killed was great, but the parents of the child who committed the killing were also at a loss. The townspeople attempted to mediate and said: "He is still a youngster who cannot judge for himself. Please forgive him." They tried in every way to placate the dead child's parents, but they would not heed the advice of the townspeople and insisted: "He must be avenged."

The dead child's mother was especially inconsolable and was prepared to go to the authorities to file a suit, but people held her back saying: "How about asking the Shintō or the Buddhist clergy to take him in as a priest so he can pray all his life for the soul of your dead son?" They attempted to reason with the parents of the dead son, but to no avail. Finally, the case was brought into court.

"He is only seven, so he probably knows nothing," His Lordship said. But the parents of the dead child replied, "He is a boy who can think of murder, so he must have been different from other children from the beginning." Then His Lordship brought out a doll and a gold coin. "Tomorrow let us have the child select one of these. If he picks up the money, it will prove that he has adult understanding and he will be executed. But if he picks up the doll, he will be spared. It will be a decision as to guilt or innocence, so be sure to bring the child tomorrow," His Lordship ordered.

All returned home, but close friends of the family whose son had committed the murder gathered together and brought forth the same type of doll that they had seen in court. They placed this next to a gold coin and warned: "If you take the gold coin, you will be killed." Threatening the child, they made him rehearse the process of choosing the doll over a hundred times that night. Even in the morning, they repeated the instructions again. Then, they took him to court.

When both parties arrived, His Lordship brought out the two objects and said, "If he takes the doll, he will be spared. But if he takes the gold coin, he will be executed." The child stepped up and took the gold coin.

"There. We told you so. See how impudent he is!" The relatives of the dead child came forward and said. The parents of the child who had committed the killing were dumbfounded and broke into tears. But His Lordship said, "Now I know the child knows nothing. Although I warned him that his life would be taken, he naively took the gold coin. This clearly proves that he is too young to distinguish anything. Is there anything more important than life? The child will be spared." This is the sentence which was passed.

3. What He Finds Is a Dream Love-affair

Long ago in a town of the Capital along Inokuma Road, lived a merchant who dyed silk sashes and peddled them in the mountain homes in Tamba. His wife had been a low-ranking lady-in-waiting at the Imperial Palace, and the scent of blossoms still clung to her and caught the attention of all who passed.

He was a poor man, and, though leaving his wife alone caused him anxiety, he had to earn his living. He was also very jealous, and when he was about to leave on a trip he would take newt's blood and smear it on his unsuspecting wife's left elbow. This "newt indicator," as it was called, left a sign a woman could not wash off as long as she refrained from relations with a man. What amorous man of long ago invented this?

In the same town as the merchant lived a young man-about-town who saw the wife and fell in love with her but had no opportunity to tell her so. She was also attracted to him. One night she dreamed she was lying beside him. The same night he dreamed that he had slipped into her home and exchanged lover's vows with her.

They both felt this to be a mysterious dream, and the man babbled about it carelessly in places where young men gathered and talked. It was a dream romance and made people laugh heartily. It takes all kinds!

Then her husband came back from Tamba, looked for his love test— the newt indicator—and found not a trace of it. His suspicion was aroused, he mauled her about and strenuously interrogated her. (She was his wife, after all, and he had his rights!)

His wife sadly protested her innocence and told him everything that had happened to her while she was away, calling on all the gods as her witness. She even told him about the dream. This inflamed the husband's suspicions even more, for the man-about-town was a handsome man.

Then, when he made inquiries, from everywhere he went he heard about the man's dream romance.

"Word of their affair got around," the husband thought, "and they spread this to throw me off the scent." This was something that should be looked into, he decided, even though people called it a "dream romance." "It is unbearable to have people say that your wife has slept with another man. My wife says she met him in a dream, but that doesn't make me feel better. They must be having a love affair." With that he went to His Lordship.

All parties were called in, and their stories heard. "There is no evidence of an immoral act," His Lordship said. "Yet to talk about sleeping with another man's wife, even in jest, was going too far. And the wife should not have talked about it even as a dream. Any stupid man would entertain suspicions under these circumstances. Let us find out whether it was a dream or a real illicit relation."

With that His Lordship had two silver receptacles brought in. He then had some blood from one of the woman's fingers squeezed into both receptacles. Then he had blood from her husband's finger squeezed into one receptacle and blood from the lover's finger in the other. After a time he studied the result.

The blood of the husband and wife had blended into one. The blood of the lover lay in a line separate from the blood of the wife. Thus His Lordship had demonstrated that the union of the two had not been consummated, and thus, it is said, by a special investigation he had dispelled a husband's doubts and reunited him with his wife as if nothing had happened.

4. The Sickle Unreturned

Long ago, a man of Ōhara village came to a town of the Capital selling brushwood. He had made several trips on the same day carrying wood to a drinking establishment in Banochō in Sanjō, but on his last trip he left behind his trusty sickle. The people in the emporium found the mountain dweller's speech amusing, and thinking it would be fun to hear his puzzled questions, took the sickle and hid it.

When the woodseller came back looking for his sickle and was told it wasn't there, he started shouting: "Sickle thieves! In broad daylight! If you don't bring it back, I'll report it and make trouble for you."

"We're not wardens of your sickle," they said and, failing to produce it, started a great furor.

Without a second thought, the woodseller rushed into the magistrate's office and told all. The owner of the bar was called in and asked about the sickle. He said only: "I don't know a thing about it."

His Lordship then said, "I'd like to look at this," and with that removed the proprietor's coat and had him wait outside. Then he sent a messenger out the back door on an errand to the proprietor's home.

"The owner of this coat wants the sickle which was hidden a little while ago; take this coat as surety," the messenger said to the man's wife. With that he handed over the coat.

The wife did not know the man, but since the coat was undoubtedly her husband's, complete with the crests of three pink stars and sword-shaped water caltrops, she took the sickle from an inner storeroom and gave it to him. He took it to the court.

Both parties were then called before His Lordship. He had five sickles brought forth and said: "Is your sickle among these?"

Without so much as touching them, the woodseller said: "It is this one."

"Take it," His Lordship said, "but be more careful about it in the future. It is, after all, the tool by which you make your living and is as important to you as is his sword and dagger to the samurai. If you come back again telling me someone has taken it, I'll have to punish you."

"As for the bar proprietor, you seem to have hidden the sickle as a joke and then did not bring it out as soon as you should have. As a result you have broken the peace of your town and made trouble for yourself. You have wasted much time because of a foolish whim. Things like this are common in society. Inform your employees, down to the lowest one, to avoid things like this in the future." Thus, it is said, he passed sentence.

5. Capital Mistresses

Long ago in a town of the Capital lived a highly prosperous merchant. After his wife died he remarried the loveliest woman of good lineage he could find; he placed her in his middle mansion and visited her from time to time. He willed his upper mansion to the fourteen-year-old son of his first wife and delegated all matters related to it to servants. Then he built himself a number of villas.

In the Flower-viewing Villa in Higashiyama he installed a mistress named Hayama. In the villa from which he watched the moon in Saga he installed a mistress named Akino. In a cool villa near the Kamo River, he

installed a mistress named Yūgure. In the Snow-viewing Villa in Kita-
yama he installed a mistress named Matsuzaki. On Kantan's pillow he
could view the beauty of four seasons in one day.[1]

Thus, without deciding till the time came where he would sleep, he
rode in his palanquin from one to the other and indulged himself in all
the pleasures the world holds. He was particularly immoderate in his love
of *sake,* to the extent that a year could go by without his knowing a sober
moment. Then, in the prime of his manhood he contracted a serious illness and died.

He left a box filled with documents spelling out very carefully what
was to be done after his death. All were present when it was opened, but
what they heard was not at all what they expected: First, my wife: since
she has no children, provision is to be made for her to move after her
retirement to the mansion in Chōja-chō. From the main estate she is to
receive enough to maintain well ten servants. She is also to receive a be-
quest of 1,000 pieces of silver.

"Next, each of my mistresses has borne me a daughter. To my twelve-
year-old daughter, I bequeath one hundred *kamme* of silver and a well-
located mansion. To my second daughter, now eleven years old, I bequeath eighty *kamme* of silver and a corner mansion. To my third
daughter, now ten years old, I bequeath fifty *kamme* of silver and a mansion. To my fourth daughter, now eight, I leave all my remaining possessions, from the ashes in the hearth to the fallen leaves in the garden. My
son, however, will have the mansion in Muromachi and two hundred
kamme."

There was another document in which he left something for his various
relatives and all the servants. It was in his own handwriting and clearly
bore his seal.

"We are ready to accept what the will directs," said the relatives of the
youngest daughter. The servants, however, did not agree to this and demurred about handing anything over.

The townspeople murmured: "When there is a son and heir in existence, a will like this is not right." Public opinion in general was so op-
posed to the will that the family and servants held a conference on the
matter and then filed suit with His Lordship.

All the parties mentioned in the will as well as the town functionaries
present when it was read were called in. "This parent was deranged,"
said His Lordship. "The document is, as we see it, a scrap of paper.[2] The
town officials, the family, and the servants should get together and with
the assistance of men of probity of the Capital discuss the matter for
twenty days. They should come to a judgment completely devoid of fa-
voritism."

All returned home and then consulted with each other from dawn till dusk until reaching an accord. They wrote down their findings and reported them: "The son, child of the legal wife, is now only fourteen years of age and has never acted against the will of his parents. As Your Lordship has pointed out, his father was given to overindulgence in sake, and without doubt the will was written under those conditions.

"We recommend that responsibility for the estate be vested with the son and heir and that the widow remain in the same house and look after him. The older three daughters should receive the legacies the will mentioned. The disposition of the estate which our late master directed, we believe, should be followed. Though the youngest daughter has been left too much, in our opinion, since her father loved her so much as to leave her the bulk of his estate and his family name, we ask that his wishes be carried out."

His Lordship had written an opinion on the matter, and when he read it and compared it with the other there was not the slightest difference. All were amazed at this. "This is the way I ask you to carry it out; may you act so that this house prospers," said His Lordship. And thus, it is said, he ordered.

6. Capital People on Pilgrimage— Blossoms on Dead Branches

Long ago from the towns of the Capital, masses of the devout would go on pilgrimage deep into the mountains by Matsunō.[1] An itinerant priest built a hut there and gained the reputation that he could cure all illnesses within seventeen days. As time went on more huts of worship were put up and even miracles proclaimed: the lame went home walking, the mute could speak, the deaf could hear men's words. He came to be compared with Yakushi, the god of medicine.

Day and night people came by the mountain; valleys were filled with their torn sandals. Yet the money changers there warned each other about the inflation of exchange rates: "It's because the donations are staying here, you know."

Once the priest said: "I have a great boon I would ask of the heavens; it is for the good of all sentient beings. What I ask is that the trees of this mountain lose their leaves and then next spring grow green with leaves again." Just as he asked the branches as far as the eye could see went bare. Some very wise men lost their doubts about him and looked up to him; the stupid ones shed even more tears of wonder.

The priest, however, was a charlatan. All the miraculously cured sick

people were shills in his employ. He was watching for the proper moment
to make off with the offerings he had received. The mountain villagers
had no complaint to make, but the villagers in the foothills came to him
saying: "Last year we used the trees from this mountain to build a bridge
off the seacoast highway, but now they are all dying, and we don't know
how to proceed in the future. Won't you use your magical powers to re-
store them?" Under pressure from great numbers of farmers, the priest
wanted to leave immediately but could not make the arrangements he
wanted for the offertory funds. At any rate, while he was scheming
about what to do, he was called by His Lordship.

The priest and the villagers were called in. After the details just given
were explained to him His Lordship said: "The plants and trees take
heart and grow bright with blossoms in great profusion. Branches grow
thick and naturally enrich the nation. There is no reason that one should
make young trees wither. You were once a doctor and now wish to use
your talents as a corrupt priest. By this I mean that you learned somewhere how to put cinnamon under the bark of trees so they would lose
their leaves. You are a criminal working to the detriment of society with
a useless, attention-getting skill. You should be executed, but since you
have taken the step of leaving the world your life will be spared. Have
him stripped naked and driven from the Ki area."[2]

"Count the offering funds precisely and place them in the care of the
nine neighboring villages. They should be able to build roads and bridges
that will last a long time," he said.

As His Lordship predicted, the priest, it is said, made his way thereafter to Yamada in Ise,[3] where he lived by taking pulses.[4]

7. A Contrivance Cast
on the Waters
of the Katsura River

Long ago, when the towns of the Capital were tranquil and word of
unusual things was not to be heard, people waited expectantly for something to which they could say, "What's that?" Then, in the current of
the Katsura River,[1] muddy with the waters of the rainy season, a strange
thing came floating.

It was a newly fashioned casket, locked and bearing a white Shintō
decoration.[2] A certain villager saw it and came calling everyone he could
find. They could not understand what the casket signified, and since they

could not leave the matter unsolved, someone suggested that, since it seemed to be connected with Shintō, that they inquire of the Yoshida or Hagiwara families.[3] Someone else suggested it would be quicker if they went to His Lordship. This they decided to do, carrying the casket there and explaining matters to him in detail with great seriousness.

He ordered first that they open the lock, and when he looked in he found five ancient skulls imbedded in a mass of women's black hair. The onlookers were shocked, looked at each other with mystified faces, and said: "What can this be?"

His Lordship said, without investigating any further: "Was this chest discovered by only one person or by a crowd?"

One man came forward and said: "I discovered it; I was alone."

"You scoundrel, you have found something useless and created a disturbance among the people of the village. To make amends, go to Shijō Kawara and tell them that any one who starts talking about a casket floating in the Katsura River in a *kyōgen* or *jōruri* play will be severely punished.[4] Announce this in the middle of performances." This was the end of the matter.

This was something contrived by actors for an incident related to a *kyōgen* play. They had retained the lone villager to float the casket in the Katsura River. His Lordship had caught on quickly and disposed of the matter quietly. The casket was displayed in a cemetery chapel. There the five skulls, of no one knows what antiquity, attracted an unexpected number of fervent prayers.

8. A Brazen Servant Reveals His Own Foulness

Long ago, in a town of the Capital, there was a man who owned a stationery store. He was not married and had only one employee, but he worked assiduously at his business and gradually his financial position became secure. Taking his lack of a wife as a blessing, the young men of the town made a hangout of his home, which resounded constantly with *kouta* and *jōruri* songs.

It was on a day later in the year than December 20; his lone servant had been gone to Ōtsu on an errand since noon, and the master impatiently awaited his return. He heard the bell strike midnight. People had long since settled quietly to sleep. Then he heard a knock at the door, and thinking it was his man came forward and opened up.

It was the son of a millionaire who lived nearby in the same town. He was a handsome boy of twenty-two or twenty-three. He seemed extremely tired. "Let me rest a little bit, and then I'll go home," he said, and pillowed his head on an account book.

He was intoxicated beyond his powers of control. "Have you been to the gay quarters again?" the homeowner asked. "Why don't you go home?" The young man did not answer.

After a time the young man awoke and said: "How unspeakable! I have been robbed of two hundred *ryō* of gold pieces. It will be terrible if people hear of this. It's an awful thing, isn't it?" His eyes narrowed, his hands and legs trembled, then his pulse ceased.

"Take this," the homeowner said, trying to give him something to revive him, but his jaw was set; even water would not pass.

Time went by; he stood there undecisively. He dared not awaken the neighbors. For a time he found the misfortune that had befallen him more than he could stand. He was bewildered and baffled and quite tired of waiting for his manservant to come home.

Finally, to his joy, the man returned. First he apprized him of what had happened from beginning to end. "If I told this to people, they would suspect me; and I would find it hard to defend myself. But no one knows about it, so please get rid of the body," he pleaded.

The servant agreed with him, "Good idea," he said and left the body in front of the parents' gate.

When day came the lamentation of the parents brought the entire town to their side. They told questioners they were completely unaware of their son's movements of the day before. "How uncertain is human life," people said and with heavy hearts reported all they knew to the authorities.

He was a person never known even to argue with anyone else; we did not dream that someone so much as had a grudge against him," said his bewildered parents. "Perhaps he was seen to have money in his pockets and a thief did this, but there are no knife marks on his body. There are no signs of blows."

"We are approaching the end of the year," His Lordship said, "and no one has a day to spare. First, take care of the body." An investigation was carried out, but nothing turned up.

The stationery merchant went about saying things like: "How transient is this floating world." And thus he kept his mouth shut during the seventy-five days in which rumors are supposed to "fly."[1] Death had undone the young man.

Afterward, the stationer's wealth steadily grew. He engaged many more servants, of both sexes. The manservant mentioned earlier, however, grew more and more overbearing. He took the same liberties as the stationer himself, always making new employees think: "He must be a relative or something the way he talks." But then they would find out it was not so.

The public at large would laugh and say: "He lets him get away with too much." Since the incident when the master had asked the servant to do him that favor, however, the master had borne it all.

In his arrogance the man would say things like, "I am responsible for the master's life," each time freezing his employer's heart within him. People in their ignorance believed that he was still going about acting as if he were the only person in the master's service.

Then the stationer purchased a rental home, completely furnished. The servant noticed this and announced that he would like to have something like it for his own home. His employer was taken aback and quietly offered as much as two hundred *kamme* as a substitute. The man was adamant. "If you don't give me this house," he said, "I shall tell about the crime back then."

Filled with dismay, the stationer promptly took steps to sign over to the man the house that was just bought. When he asked the town authorities for permission, they demurred: "Although there may not seem to be anything wrong with giving away something that belongs to one, the person receiving it must be screened by us.[2] We did not wholeheartedly permit even you to buy the home. It is all the more difficult for us to treat as an equal a man who, up until today, has been a servant of yours. Indeed, that he is a prospective owner goes beyond our expectations. Although you may wish to give him the property, don't expect him to be allowed to participate in the town council." The townspeople were as one in opposition.

The stationer found their attitude to be reasonable and tried as well as he could to impress his opinion on the servant who would have none of it. "Surely there is no record of anyone's being prevented from receiving what his master had given him," he said, in great anger, and took up the matter with higher authorities.

"As the town authorities say," said His Lordship, "the master is neither stupid nor moribund, but I would like him to tell me the reason that he is giving such a handsome house to his servant, and I would like that man to tell me why he feels he has a right to accept it. Of course, I have my own opinion on the matter."

The magistrate did not concern himself with the testimony from the townspeople but concentrated his investigation around his suspicions in the case. He told the two men if they did not explain matters fully they would be tortured. Feeling he had no other recourse, the manservant told all, claiming innocence to save himself. The master explained in detail how he was not responsible for the man's death. After hearing their pleas, His Lordship came to the conclusion that they were not guilty of homicide. "Yet," said His Lordship, "you failed to report the matter to the authorities and also abandoned the corpse, offenses that can, under no circumstances, be ignored." Thus, it is said, although the signboards stated that they had not committed murder, they were executed.

9. Biwa[1] Music Reveals a Clue

Long ago in a town of the Capital the weather was hotter than usual. People were impatient for sundown and found cool spots on the river plain, washed off the sweat of the day in the water, and enjoyed themselves listening to the sound of the stream. Some made pleasing music; others drank *sake* with the women; the mountain monks passed by with their young acolytes. There were tens of thousands of people congregated about, yet there was not a single word of dissatisfaction.

Then, when one might have been brought to admire the hearts of the people of Kyōto, a rough group of Hokkoku samurai encountered a powerful band of Kantō men. Before one could say a fight was on, bloody swords flashed. After a short exchange, three men on the one side, including their leader, were slain. It seemed certain that their attackers numbered five or six, but they all had fled, not without wounds. A number of innocent bystanders had received sword cuts before the band, as if drunk, staggered from the scene. The events were reported by eyewitnesses in the teahouses on the riverbank.

In the morning an innkeeper informed the authorities. They were thus able to get some information, but though they instituted an investigation of the killers they found out little.

Then two brothers related to the Hokkoku band came to Kyōto on leave from their positions and filed petitions for a vendetta.[2] They were sixteen and nineteen, young and fierce, but they knew neither the faces nor the identities of their enemies. "This is a terrible thing," they said, "with your sympathetic assistance and permission to seek out and ascertain the identity of our enemies, we shall succeed in our endeavor." His Lordship was receptive to their fervent pleas, and the search began.

First, all the surgeons in the Capital were notified: "If you have treated anyone for sword wounds since the eleventh of June, please inform us in writing today. Anyone found concealing this information will be punished."

Upon receiving the notice, Yanagida Kenzan, a surgeon noted for his skill, who lived near Kōdō in Ichijōji, appeared before His Lordship. He said: On the evening of the 12th of last month, before 10 P.M., a man who looked like a farm laborer came to my home carrying a lantern with a flower-cart design. He said he worked for a village headman in Mibu and was sent to get my help. He said that the village headman had never met me before but asked for my services for his abscess was causing much discomfort. He apologized for the trouble he was causing me and asked if I would go with him to see the man.

"Considering this to be part of my duty as a physician, I put a medicine box under my garment and went with him to a country road. There, in the shade of some pines, a palanquin approached. He called it over and asked me to get in. Thinking this would be of help to my aging legs I did so.

"Suddenly a mob of men poured out of the bamboo grass, snapped a lock on the palanquin, and took me perhaps east or perhaps south. It was a zigzag trail, designed to confuse my memory. It was like a dream as we left the Capital.

"When we had gone about six miles, the footsteps about me quieted down. There was a sound as of a gate being opened. I was carried down a long corridor, and then the palanquin door was opened and I got out.

"All I could see was the reflection from a gold screen; I thought I would die on the spot. I lost consciousness for a bit; I seemed to be hearing voices in a dream. Then a heavily bearded man appeared saying: 'We have brought you here to help us because my master avoids society. Have no fear.'

"With that he opened a sliding door. Inside were six men lying about with various wounds, creating a very disturbing scene. Given the circumstances, I could not say no. So I treated them there for twenty days, under lamplight day and night, never seeing the light of day and above all not the rest of the house. When they were on the road to recovery I was given ten pieces of silver as payment and warned that if I told anyone what had happened there I would pay for it with my life. I simply asked the heavens that I might get home safely.

"I got into the palanquin again and was left in the same desolate spot from which I departed. Since then I have been quite ill and have delayed reporting the matter."

"Did the place seem to be a mountain dwelling?" he was asked.

"As you surmise, sir, it was far from the settlements. The birds there were very noisy. It seemed to be a house isolated from others. Through the open window I could see a high mountain. I asked what mountain it was and was told it was Mount Asahi."

"It wasn't the Mount Asahi in Uji; probably it was the one in Kita-yama. Do you remember anything else?"

"From the south side, or at least the side the moon shone from, I could hear biwa music; one doesn't hear it much in the Capital. I have turned a hand a little to this instrument and therefore know it was played well. What's more, on the twelfth day after I had left home, meaning on the 23rd, I could hear voices of crowds of people over on that mountain. That's all I remember."

"That must have been near Saga," said His Lordship. "The voices at dawn on the 24th were from pilgrims at Mount Atago."

He warned the surgeon to say nothing to anyone about the incident and sent him home. Then he called in all the biwa priests in the Capital and asked: "Have any of you been called recently to perform a biwa concert near Saga?"

A blind biwa player named Kikusaki came forward and said: "Once in a while I'm asked to play the biwa for the *rōnin* group near Saga. Their leader is a man over seventy who indulges in it as a sop to his age, and he has acknowledged my help with that. He has a group of *rōnin* for neighbors; but they have been sick lately. He hasn't wished to bother them and so has stopped having concerts."

"I have a few more questions to ask you," said His Lordship. "Do not talk to the others about them."

Soon His Lordship called in some of the residents of Saga and made inquiries of them. "Our neighbors certainly look like *rōnin*," one answered. "They rented a house early in May and were indulging in all kinds of games there every day, but since the middle of June they have been said to be sick and even the servant samurai don't appear."

Believing this to be the answer, His Lordship summoned the brothers from Hokkoku, and told them: "Look into this matter carefully, and then attack, if you wish."

They thanked His Lordship and made their way to west Saga. There they made very discreet inquiries and determined that these men were indeed participants in the battle on the river plain on the night of June 11th. They set the hundredth day after the fight as the day for action and then, with five retainers, attacked the house. Announcing their names as they swung their swords, they killed all the men, leaving no survivors.

Then they reported what they had done to His Lordship, said prayers for their father at Nison-in, a temple in Saga, placed the heads of their enemies in containers for evidence for the people at home, and returned to Hokkoku with feet firmly on the path of the warrior.[3]

NOTES TO PART IV

1. A WISE WOMAN'S FIB

1. When a male child becomes three, a special rite is performed on November 15 of the lunar calendar. The top part of the child's head is shaved (*kamioki* in Japanese).

2. Festival of the dead is held on July 15 of the lunar calendar. Many types of delicacies are offered to the spirit of the ancestors. By bestowing food to famished ghosts (Sanskrit, *preta;* Japanese, *gaki*) in inferno, one is able to pray for the repose of one's ancestors' souls and save them from suffering.

2. TWO CHOICES: ONE GOOD, ONE BAD

1. The Gion Festival, related to the Yasaka Shrine of Kyōto, was formerly held on June 7 of the lunar calendar but today it is observed between July 17 and 24. This festival is famous for its parade of *dashi* (tall carts used as floats).

4. THE SICKLE UNRETURNED

In *Itakura seiyō*, Zokuhen, Vol. 9, Shoshidai Shigemune solves a case of a lost sickle. A similar story is in Anrakuan Sakuden's *Seisuishō*, 4, 7.

5. CAPITAL MISTRESSES

1. In the *Cheng Chung Chi,* written by Li Pi, a man borrowed a wish-granting pillow and dreamed that he became a successful and wealthy man. Then he awoke to find that what took a lifetime in his dream lasted only a brief spell in real life. Saikaku mentions Kantan's dream because the man in the story could visit the four villas (representing four seasons) of his mistresses in one day, thus enjoying all the pleasures of the four seasons in that short time.

2. If a will made by a person on his deathbed is irrational, it becomes null and void.

6. CAPITAL PEOPLE ON PILGRIMAGE—BLOSSOMS ON DEAD BRANCHES

This story resembles two stories in *T'ang Ying Pi Shih,* nos. 47 and 48, in which evil priests try to take money by deception.

1. Location is in Kasa county, Yamashiro province (Kyōto). Matsuo Shrine exists at the foot of these mountains.

2. Ki area. Yamashiro (Kyōto prefecture), Yamato (Nara prefecture), Kawachi (Ōsaka prefecture), Izumi (Ōsaka prefecture) and Settsu (Ōsaka and Hyōgo prefectures).

3. Ise is in present-day Mie prefecture. It is famous for the Ise Shrine, enshrining Amaterasu, the Sun Goddess.

4. A nonprofessional medical examiner.

7. A CONTRIVANCE CAST ON THE WATERS OF THE KATSURA RIVER

1. Katsura River flows through Ukyō Ward, Kyōto. It is the downstream of the Ōi River, which combines with the Kamo River, then meets the Uji River, and finally combines with the Yodo River (in Ōsaka prefecture).

2. White strips of paper offered at shrines (in Japanese, *hei, hakuhei, nusa,* or *mitegura*).

3. Yoshida was the family connected with the Yoshida Shrine and Hagiwara was a branch family of the Yoshida.

4.   Shijō Kawara is the riverbank between Sanjō and Shijō of the Kamo River. This area was famous during this period for its puppets and kabuki theaters.

8. A BRAZEN SERVANT REVEALS HIS OWN FOULNESS

This story resembles *T'ang Ying Pi Shih,* no. 55; a man moves a corpse to another's gate to put the suspicion on his neighbor.

1.   This was a popular saying of this period.
2.   Elders of the *gonin-gumi* ("five-man group," incorporated during the Tokugawa Period as a means of checks and balances) examined whether the acquisition of a home befitted one's status.

9. BIWA MUSIC REVEALS A CLUE

1.   A Japanese lute.
2.   Vendettas could be carried out legally if permission was granted by magistrates or by higher authorities.
3.   *Bushidō,* the moral code of the warrior class, began from the end of the twelfth century. It emphasized loyalty, sacrifice, fidelity, courteousness, humility, integrity, militarism, honor, affection, and so on.

Part V
FORGIVENESS

1. Palace Prints Covered with Cherry Blossoms

Long ago in a town of the Capital lived a man who became rich almost overnight. In this world, so chary about offering a decent living, this man, thanks to his wife's wisdom, hung up the shingle of marriage broker. They searched about the Capital throughout the year for prospects, and finally girls of marriageable age began coming to this couple with their mothers. The mothers would show off their daughters, tell their ages, and determine the dowry they were prepared to pay. Young men also applied to this couple for brides equal in status. The matchmakers listened to both parties and arranged matters skilfully so there would be no complaints later on. Thus many people throughout the towns of the Capital came to them to have their marriages arranged. Such an unusual occupation became accepted.

Their fee was paid by the groom, and amounted to one-tenth of the dowry.

One day in late autumn they were returning from viewing the maple leaves at Tsūten Bridge,[1] when they passed a fashionable young woman in a fetching palace print *kimono* with long sleeves. On a scale of beauty she would have rated somewhere between average and better than average. She was accompanied by someone who looked like her mother and a number of woman servants. Though they were not from their neighborhood, the matchmakers approached them and asked about the girl.

"We don't expect to marry her to a man of high rank, but we shall give a dowry of two hundred pieces of silver. If money is not asked by the other party, we could lay that out in wearing apparel. We leave it to the groom and his family. Now that I have talked this over with you so confidentially, we will do everything as you say.

"She doesn't have the best breeding, and she isn't as intelligent as other daughters. She would probably not be suitable for a merchant. She might do for a physician without family who has recently come from the country, or perhaps an unpunctilious priest of the Pure Land True sect.[2] All we ask is a home where she will not be noticed," said the lady.

"How old is she?" asked the matchmaker.

"Going on eighteen," was the answer.

"My, you are an upright parent! Nowadays, people falsify ages by seven or eight years, but let us just say she is sixteen."

"I'm not concerned about the world hereafter," the woman said, "but I don't like falsehoods of that kind. Let's say outright she is eighteen. After all, the other party will check the horoscopes. This floating world does not last long; it is futile to hide one's age. Please state the truth.

"She does not have a scar on her body, not so much as the scratch of a feather. On the tip of her left shoulder are two small moles. Other than that, her body has no abnormality." After stripping the girl naked as it were with her words, she left.

The couple heard these words marveling that there could still be a parent like this. They accepted the charge and soon took up the matter with a suitable man of the same religious sect. He found it most felicitous that the wife should be pretty and have a dowry too and quickly agreed. An auspicious date was selected and the palanquin with its retinue of maids was brought to the home of the groom and placed in the inner room. Then, lo and behold, when the serving women looked at the bride in the candlelight, they discovered she had only one eye!

Shocked by what the servants had told her, the matchmaker's wife looked under the cotton veil and saw a girl about two years older than the one she had seen earlier. She had been shown the younger sister and then had the older sister pulled over her! "In all the years I have been in this business, this is the first time I have been hoodwinked. I was careless, and now I have lost face. I shall do something about it!"

The parents of the groom observed the chagrin and the anger of the matchmaker's wife without any outward show of concern. "If they want to make a fool of someone," they said, "we can play the same game. Our oldest son was left mute by illness, and we have not permitted him to take his place in society; but now let us bring him forth and marry him off! She with her one eye and he speechless will make a match no one will be able to complain about." With that the ritual sake was drunk.[3]

After five days the bride paid a visit to her parents. When she told them about her husband, they clapped their hands in astonishment. They recognized, however, that they had erred in the matter and out of deference to public opinion said nothing; but they did not send the girl back. They tried to recover the dowry, but the groom's family refused. Words were exchanged and the matter became quite unpleasant. Then the matchmakers, provoked with the bride's parents, brought the matter to a head with a lawsuit.

His Lordship heard the complaint and called in both parties. "This event began because of the evil intentions of the bride's parents. It was fortunate for both sides that the prospective groom had a defective brother. It would be best now if these two parties already related herewith marry the daughter that was discussed at that earlier time with the sound younger brother. The same matchmakers will serve for this union.''

The families expressed their gratefulness and departed. The matchmakers were particularly delighted.

"The reason for the difficulty with the older daughter's wedding," they said, "was that it was held after dark. So let us have the younger sister married not in the dark but in daylight.''[4] And so it was done, to the great amusement of the Capital.

2. An Order to Pile Up Four or Five Bowls

Long ago, in a town of the Capital, while everyone was busy preparing for the New Year, pounding *mochi* and dusting away soot under the December sky, a seller of rice bowls came down from his mountain home in Tamba and, since he did not know his way around the city, put down his bundle of wares by the Gion shrine and looked around at things like the *ema* lamplighting charm.[1] A man in country costume observed him, picked up his bundle, and ran off.

The bowl vendor ran after him and pursued him out the South Gate. Somehow he managed to apprehend him near the Yasaka tower. "How dare you steal a man's belongings in broad daylight?" he shouted.

The thief, to his dismay, shouted the same complaints, and though the residents of the area gathered in great numbers they found it difficult to determine the rightful owner. The statements made by the two men did not help them arrive at the answer. "One of them is the thief," the residents said, and surrounding the men they took them to His Lordship.

He listened to the men's stories, which were identical. Then he had the bundle of bowls unpacked and the contents distributed in the courtyard, after which he told the men he wanted them to race at piling up bowls. When he called the signal the men started. While one man piled up four or five bowls, the other swept all the rest into a tall pile in his hands.

The thief was exposed. He was stripped naked and expelled from the city. The bowl vendor, it is said, was given the thief's clothing.

3. Pulse-taking Priest
Thumps a Thief

Long ago in a town of the Capital, lived an artisan who made umbrellas designed for the northern country. He had many apprentices, and gradually his livelihood improved and his family name, Tsuboya, became well known. Bad weather was good luck to this family.

One night when the spring rain was falling without letup, the master gave his many apprentices time off to compensate them for their recent exertions along with some of the famous sake called "Uji River." As they drank to their heart's content, the master in high spirits sang a *kouta* he did rather poorly and his apprentices intoned a *jōruri*. Soon it was past midnight, and they all fell asleep without bothering about going to bed. His wife went around, as usual, making sure everything was taken care of. She checked that the gates were closed, made sure the locks had been fastened at dusk to keep intruders from entering during the night, and then retired.

The next morning they woke later than usual. When the master rose, however, he looked for but could not find two *kamme* of silver which he had received from a wholesaler the night before and had placed before the safe. He made various inquiries about it but was unable to locate the money.

The matter was reported to the town councillors, who conferred and rendered the opinion that the thief could not have come in from the outside since the gate was locked and there was no other entrance. The money must have been taken by one of the twelve apprentices. A quiet investigation was decided upon, and a complaint was filed.

The entire household was summoned into court and interrogated, but the apprentices were so frightened by His Lordship that after their depositions were taken so many as three of them were suspect. As the interrogation grew more intense they began to shake and grow red in the face and lost the ability to reply to the questioning. At this rate the investigation would have grave difficulty continuing. Some people are congenitally susceptible to being frightened by the slightest occurrence, while others remain unmoved even in mortal peril.

"It is not proper to torture people who are innocent," the law officers said, pondering how best to come at this case. Then His Lordship ordered that they should alter the method of investigation, and he summoned his family physician. "Please take the pulses of the apprentices, and if anyone's pulse rate is not normal report it to me without equivocation," he said and quietly had the doctor installed in a separate room.

Then the twelve apprentices were lined up and told: "One of you stole the money; we will now torture you until he confesses." Then they were taken in order of seniority into the room. Even those who were innocent had lost much of their composure by this time. Their pulse rates, however, were unchanged. There was one apprentice who seemed perfectly calm and his testimony above suspicion, but his pulse was nevertheless unusually rapid, in fact, nearly unable to bear the strain. This fact was reported to His Lordship.

The man was severely interrogated and confessed the crime, going as far as revealing the whereabouts of the silver and apologizing for the trouble he had caused. Then the master of the shop pleaded in behalf of the apprentice: "Though he worked with the apprentices, he is in fact a nephew of my former wife and therefore quite different from them, in fact, practically a son of the family. I have even planned to will our family name to him. What he did was the same as stealing his own property, so I beg that you show mercy and pardon his crime. I suggest you allow him to become a monk."

As the shop owner requested, the life of the apprentice was spared. His Lordship passed sentence saying: "He is an evildoer who has caused trouble to many people, so he must take the tonsure. Give him an umbrella which he made himself and expel him from the house."

4. Without Two Parties Present the Storehouse Does Not Open

Long ago in a town of the Capital, there was a wholesaler who dealt in ornamental heads for sword hilts. He married a girl from Naniwa and lived happily with her for eleven years. Then, when his son was seven years of age, he died. Since the man felt that his wife was resigned to become a widow, he bequeathed all his wealth to his wife and child and specified that until his son became eighteen the shop would be managed by the head servant and that the annual report would be rendered in the presence of the boy's paternal and maternal relatives.

Besides the stock for the business, there was five thousand *ryō* of gold, which the paternal parents suggested they should take custody of until the child was eighteen. The maternal relatives, however, said that they should be the custodians. The families were suspicious of each other, and since they could not settle the argument themselves, they decided to go to His Lordship and explain the problem.

His Lordship found the arguments of both parties quite reasonable and handed down the following ruling: "The relatives and the town councillors should ascertain the value of the gold coins, and when the value is confirmed, should store the sum carefully in the inner vault. The lock of the wooden door should be sealed by the paternal relatives. The earthen door should bear the seal of the maternal relatives. The key to the wooden door should be entrusted to the maternal relatives, and the key for the mud door to the paternal relatives. Then, when the son becomes eighteen, he should be given the keys. Care of the storehouse will be entrusted to the head servant."

This was the solution which dispelled all lingering suspicions, and all gratefully accepted it. Everyone greatly admired His Lordship for devising a vault which could not be opened without the presence of two parties.

5. A Life Hangs upon the Tip of a Writing Brush

Long ago in a town of the Capital, there lived a man who had been a samurai. Having accumulated much gold and silver, he had resigned from the services of his lord, and went with his wife to live the life of a townsman near the Iwagami Shrine. He had a son who was very handsome and excelled at all the educated arts. He was especially skillful at writing and taught calligraphy.

After his parents died, however, he indulged himself with harlots night and day, until his money was all gone and he had to sell his household goods, but even that did not turn him from his ways.

In all his dallyings, he patronized the same high-ranking courtesan. For seven years he had been her lover, and the geisha did not forget his affection of all those months and years. Even when his fortune was gone, her regard for him did not waver.

One day, he decided to help her leave the brothel by illegal means. It was a moonless, rainy night in May, so dark that even if he had his nose pinched, he could not see who did it. He, with four or five of his friends as accomplices, quietly carried out the lady in a coffin covered in a white sheet. The guard at the main gate witnessed this and remarked: "This is the way of all mortals. I wonder whose grandmother this is?" The sight made him feel the transience of life.

When, later that night, it was discovered that the belle of the brothel had disappeared, the watchman at the main gate was questioned and said: "During the night, I left my post only once, and that was on an errand for a penny-pinching brothel owner who had run out of sake. Other than a coffin someone carried out for burial, not so much as a rat got out."

"Ah ha," the searchers thought, and inquired at all the other brothels, but there was no report of a funeral. "No doubt someone sneaked her out in this way," the brothel keeper said. The attendants who were with the courtesan were questioned, but no information could be obtained.

Then the letters of the courtesan were examined. She had been very careful at the beginning to dispose of everything which might give a clue, but it was her ill fate to leave one letter without a return address under the *tatami*. In the letter were all the details of the plot to carry her out of the gay quarters. The handwriting on the letters was studied and found to be unmistakably that of the former samurai. With this as evidence, a complaint naming him was filed with the authorities.

The man was summoned into Court and asked: "Is this your handwriting?"

"No, Your Lordship," he replied; "it is not."

"Then," said His Lordship, "Write the same words as this letter."

The *rōnin* had a fine grasp of the art of handwriting and wrote for the magistrate in a hand quite different from that he normally used. His Lordship looked at the result and said: "From the differences in the handwriting I see here, what you say is true. But judging by letters you wrote much earlier, you have deliberately introduced those differences in handwriting." With that His Lordship brought out some other letters the man had written. He pointed at them and said that there were three variations in the handwriting. Then he asked the *rōnin* to write the incriminating letter again. This time His Lordship looked only at the sentences. He saw that though the movement of the brush was different, the spacing of the characters and the way in which they were connected did not vary in the slightest from the other letters.

As the examining progressed and the *rōnin*'s complicity became more and more clear, one of his friends and coconspirators told His Lordship how the man had spent seven thousand *ryō* on the courtesan and lost his fortune. He then said: "Our friend was told that he could purchase the courtesan's freedom for two thousand *ryō*, and with your permission I shall collect that amount from my friends and we shall pay the brothel proprietor for her." The money was given to the brothel as he suggested, and thus, it is said the matter was worked out.

6. A Memory Device
Tied to the Little Finger

Long ago, in Ryōgae-machi in the Capital, many transactions were carried out every day in buying gold or smaller currency as the rate of exchange fluctuated. A group of businessmen there had an understanding that permitted freer dealing among their houses. If only a small sum of money was borrowed, the lender did not need to write a note; he would only jot it down in his memo book. Thus they carried out their business with each other.

At one time, a certain clerk borrowed ten *ryō* in gold but failed to return it after four or five days had elapsed. The young clerk who had made the loan noticed that the debt had not been erased from his book and went to collect it. The borrower, however, had erased his notation and claimed that he had returned the loan the day he had borrowed it. Then the lender totalled up all the funds he had taken in since the time of the transaction but still found himself ten *ryō* short. He was sure he had not received payment. They argued back and forth, but the matter seemed no closer to solution.

The sum was not large, but in monetary matters any sum is important, and for the sake of future business transactions it had to be explained. The masters called in their clerks and after putting everything on paper filed a suit with the authorities.

After listening to both parties, His Lordship spoke to the clerk who had borrowed the money and said: "If you cannot remember what goes on in the difficult currency transactions you must carry out, you will have much trouble. To remind you of what you have forgotten. . . ." With that His Lordship tied the little fingers of the man's hands together with a twisted paper string and stamped it with his seal. Then he allowed the clerk to return home. To the young clerk who had loaned the money, His Lordship said: "Since this was caused by carelessness, until this matter is settled you are ordered to carry a twenty-five digit abacus in one hand wherever you go." After passing this light sentence, His Lordship sent the man home.

The clerk who had his little fingers tied had been wrong in this matter from the beginning, and after having gone through the interrogation he regretted that he had caused himself and others so much inconvenience. He therefore pleaded: "It was all my carelessness; I now remember that I did not return the money."

"Since you realize your mistake, you may return the money and that will end this matter," His Lordship said, pardoning the man, we are told.

7. A Man with a Mind Manifest in Smoke

Long ago, in a town of the Capital, there lived a man who lived extravagantly and built a villa in Nawate in Sanjō which he used for amusement. He had a clerk who had been in his employ for a long time who was somewhat of a recluse and disliked going out in the city. The master made this clerk caretaker of the villa and allowed him to live there as he wished.

He still kept in his employ the nurse who had brought him up, and he had long thought about setting both her and his clerk up in a business. When he broached it to them, the nurse agreed and said: "Whatever it be, I will follow the wishes of you and your wife." But the clerk did not consent. He turned aside all efforts to persuade him. Since this was a matter of lifelong union, the employer felt he could not compel the man. The matter was left as it was, and the clerk went on living his disciplined life. People looked at him, envied him, saying: "That's a good way to live, too!"

The nurse, however, in her womanly heart resented the clerk's refusal to accept her as his wife. She plotted constantly to bring harm to the clerk, but he was an upright man, and other than going out to the temple for the memorials of his ancestors he did not venture outside the gates at night. Finding no other way open to her, she quietly got in touch with certain rough shanty dwellers.

One day she went by palanquin with the master's wife to the villa. The visit was more cheerful than usual, and they enjoyed themselves until late that night. Amid all the good cheer and the confusion of their departure, the nurse managed to unlock the gate on the river side and leave it open. She also stole the key of the storehouse and departed serenely.

The clerk was a very conscientious person and attempted to put the house in order, but because all was in such disorder he was unable to complete the task that night. About midnight, with the job almost done, he fell into bed.

That night the nurse gave the key to her hirelings and had them sneak into the home before morning and steal the *kakemono*s (hanging scrolls), the incense burners, the vases, and even the bedding. Then she gave the men some money and had them take the loot to the home of the clerk's parents. "We don't know the reason very well," they said, very persuasively, "but your son has sent these from the Capital. He will be here in four or five days." Without thinking any more about them, the parents took the goods into their custody.

The following morning, the clerk was shocked to find that the villa had been burglarized and reported the burglary to the employer. That man assayed what had been done and said: "This was not done by someone who did not know his way around the household." He then decided to investigate the matter privately.

At that time, a fearful mountain-priest called Tengu-bo was enlisted by the nurse as an accomplice in the plot.[1] She then secured the permission of her mistress to call the priest in and coached him in what he was to say. The priest was then shown the back entrance where he solemnly said: "The burglar is a member of this household," as if told by divine communication.

What he said tallied with what the master had suspected, so he said: "We would like to request your aid. Please reveal the culprit to us."

The mountain-priest agreed and said: "Give me the names of everyone living in this household as well as the names of all the servants living outside." A total of thirty-one names were listed for the priest. "This very night, I will call forth a definite sign," he said, with great certainty. "I would like all these people to sit with me tomorrow. I will then point out the culprit to you." He returned to his home that day.

The following day, at high noon, the mountain priest arrived and facing all the people gathered there said: "I will now place this paper in the smoke, and the name of the person who has done the misdeed will burn with the holy flame of Fudō (god of fire)." With that he put the list inside the smoke, and a miracle occurred—around the clerk's name appeared the halo of Fudō.

"So that's who it was," thought the master, filled with suspicion against the clerk. The clerk, innocent as he was, was greatly troubled and decided to get to the bottom of the matter.

Then the master dispatched someone to investigate the home of the clerk's parents in Kusatsu in Gōshū (Shiga prefecture), and discovered that the clerk's parents had possession of the stolen goods. Now he was convinced without doubt that the clerk was guilty and applauded the occult powers of the mountain-priest. "In normal times you'd take the clerk for a law-abiding citizen, but you can never predict what people will do," people were saying. The clerk was not able to tolerate this and filed suit against the mountain-priest.

Everyone in the household was summoned into court. His Lordship was told that all the stolen goods were in the home of the clerk's parents, but he still had reason to believe that the clerk was not guilty. He asked the mountain-priest to testify saying: "You obtained swift results with your sacred powers. Indeed, how fabulous they are!" After repeatedly commending the priest, His Lordship said, "Fortunately we too have a thief we would like you to expose. Find him for us just as you did the other.'' Then His Lordship wrote down ten names and said, ''The thief is one of these people.'' The mountain priest was perplexed but accepted the list and returned home. He prepared the same artifice as before and went again to His Lordship. Again when he held the paper in smoke, one name on the list shone clear.

His Lordship laughed out loud and said, ''If you had only said there is no thief on this list, you would have been commended. That list I gave you meant nothing. The one who made an innocent man's name appear in smoke was the guilty one.'' With that he ordered an investigation. The part played by the nurse was made clear and, it is said, the thieves soon implicated.

When his end was near the mountain priest whispered to his porter: ''This manifestation in which a word appears in smoke is a hundred years old. It is done by writing with the juice of a bitter orange and then holding the writing over a flame which will highlight it. It is a despicable trick, but with it I earned many offerings. And now I pass it on to you.'' It is said that everyone listening broke into laughter.

8. They Knew the Name but Not the Face

Long ago, in a town of the Capital, lived a man who against all advice sold everything his father had left him and day and night revelled in the amusements of the floating world. Then he fell in with companions given to dreaming up evil tricks.

Man is by nature neither wise nor evil, and this man when he was still respectable was almost too honest. In fact, out of one hundred things he said, not one was untrue. Now, however, out of one thousand things he said, not three would be true. Thus he was known as Semmitsu (three out of a thousand).

Certain traits of his former character remained, and even though clothed in paper he was one of the most handsome men of the Capital. His acquaintances therefore set him up in a rented house on an unfrequented alley and gave out his name, identical with that of a well-known family of the Capital. It was a name well known even in this neighborhood.

One day his friends had him impersonate the son of that very wealthy family, dressing him in that scion's clothing and even the crest of the family. Accompanied by a host of retainers, even to one shaved bald like a wise bailiff, he quietly visited an actor's amusement house in East Kawaramachi. Someone said to the landlord: "If you would like to become the manager, my master will advance whatever funds you require."

That man, delighted, said: "This is what I have wanted for a long time; I certainly do not intend to end up as I am now." With that he bowed three times and looked very grateful. Convivialities like "sweeping the garden with a hammer"[1] were too theatrical for them, so they made the night bright telling stories to suit current tastes.

The enterprise was kept secret from the public, but somehow the people of the theatre's "last act" heard about it, got into the house and made themselves part of the program. They brought gifts every time they came, and word got about until everybody wanted to get in. "We have heard," they said, "that you are a great lover and patron of the gay quarters, but for you to take up residence here is extraordinary. It is a good sign for the business of Kawara." Then they hung on him saying "Master, Master," in rapt admiration.

Then a man who looked like a physician appeared and whispered to the devoted followers: "The master is planning to take a trip to the eastern provinces in the spring. Please sponsor him."

Various admirers disputed over the privilege of being his sponsor, saying things like: "He can easily get a loan of ten thousand *ryō*." One went to a lender of money for houses of ill fame and mentioned the man's name. He was told: "I can lend that man up to five thousand *ryō*," and given a standard rate of interest. Another offered to lend two thousand *ryō* for one imprinting of the great man's seal.

The money was delivered to the Shingon temple in Higashiyama. The lenders inspected the great man's seal on the note and returned.

Time passed, and the money was not paid when due. The lenders were puzzled, served notice on the family, and were shocked to be told: "We don't know anything about it."

They then went to the men who had acted as mediators. They, in turn, went to visit the borrower and found that he lived in a dingy rented home. All the belongings of his household together were worth only about a hundred *me*. They decided that the man and his friends were swindlers. The man himself was unmoved. "I won't deny that I borrowed the money," he said. "The son of a famous millionaire in the Capital has the same first and last name as I, but my name is not an alias. You can check it at the town office. It is also on the lease for this house."

"In this great Capital there is nothing mysterious about two men having the same first and last names. I wondered at the time why anyone would lend so much money to such an obscure person as I. I thought it was because the mediators were so persuasive. I am the borrower, but I did not take the money, and I do not know its whereabouts. You urge me to pay the money, but the god of the Gion Shrine knows that I am penniless. The furniture here is not mine; I rented this house furnished. All that I own that is not on my back is a long bow without arrows, a book on etiquette, a nose-halter inlaid with mother of pearl, two cryptomeria nested boxes without covers, and some old letters from harlots and female-impersonators. There is no use arguing about thousands or tens of thousands. Take this that I have only one of and divide it. I have never considered it my own anyway.'' With that, he stretched out his neck. The moneylenders recovered their composure, retreated, and filed a suit with His Lordship.

His Lordship is said to have listened to the details of the case and concluded: "Whatever the circumstances, this was caused by the folly of the lenders. It happened because you turned from the normal rate of interest in favor of an exorbitant monthly interest rate of seven and a half percent.''

9. Transmitting the Noh Master's Art

Long ago in a town of the Capital, there was a man called Fushimi Dayū, who earned his livelihood as a noh master. He lived in the vicinity of the Shirakawa Bridge and performed much of the Zashiki Noh[1] that was done in the Ryōzen-Maruyama district.

At this time in the hamlet of Fushimi there was a historic place called Saigyō Temple.[2] In front of this temple was the Moon-Reflecting Pond, a famous pond whose limpid waters shone with a warm glow. In autumn, sightseers with deep aspirations to the art of poetry gathered here in great numbers to view the moon. The dew hung heavy on the bush clover in the garden. The head priest was upset that there was so little room for visitors and for years had hoped to build pavilions there, but time passed without his wish being fulfilled.

The noh master heard about this matter and was considering giving a three-day benefit noh performance in order to get these structures built. He was an old man, however, and his feet were causing him pain, so he felt constrained to put off the occasion. But among his many pupils were Yama Dayū and Kawa Dayū, as dependable as his two hands, and he decided to send them to serve in his stead.

The two pupils, however, disputed over who would perform the "Oki-

na" dance ("old man," traditionally the first play in a noh performance), and even the master's words did not settle the matter. They went
on fighting as if their lives depended on it. There were many other parts
to play, from the musician's section to the chorus, so they were advised
to draw lots and alternate daily, but they remained obdurate. All were
upset that the master's dream would not be fulfilled, when he said: "We
can't settle this matter this way; let us take it to court," and shut off all
further argument. Then everyone appeared before His Lordship.

"The basis of art is competition, and there is nothing wrong with being
self-centered about it. Now, however, in order to hand his school on to
the next generation, the master intends to teach his most secret arts to his
outstanding disciple. Let both men, therefore, now dance in a group
dance. The one who is most skillful will be given the lead role."

"Since the place where the benefit noh will be held is the Saigyō Temple, you shall both perform "Eguchi,"[3] ordered His Lordship.

Fortunately, the musicians were there, so His Lordship called for the
flutes and drums. Each *tayū* stood up in the courtyard and did his dance.
After observing them dance, His Lordship arrived at a decision.
"Though I am not an expert in this art, there was a point in which Yama
Dayū was more sensitive than Kawa Dayū. I was interested to see that
where the words went "on riding on the white clouds," Yama Dayū did
not stamp his feet. Pass on to Yama Dayū the secrets of the art and let
him perform the role of "Okina.""

It is said that in gratitude they sang: "Today's judgment shows that
'the world is at peace, and the country tranquil,' " and they left the
court.

NOTES TO PART V

1. PALACE PRINTS COVERED WITH CHERRY BLOSSOMS

1.   Tsūten Bridge is located on the grounds of the Tōfukuji Temple, Higashiyama
    Ward, Kyōto. It is about twenty-five meters long. This place was a famous spot
    for viewing maple leaves in autumn.

2.   At this time, the priests of most Buddhist sects were forbidden to marry;
    however, the Pure Land True sect, founded by Shinran (1173–1262), was an ex-
    ception.

3.   The groom and bride would drink three times respectively from a set of three
    sake cups, in Japanese, *sansankudo.*

4.   Weddings were always held in the evening; however, this is not true today.

2. AN ORDER TO PILE UP FOUR OR FIVE BOWLS

In *T'ang Ying Pi Shih,* no. 102, a cow was stolen and both owner and robber
claimed that it was his. The judge freed the animal and it returned to its owner.
Also in *T'ang Ying Pi Shih,* no. 8, two women claimed to be the mother of a

child. The judge ordered them to a tug-of-war, pulling the child by his arms; the winner would be decided the mother. His real mother lost because she pitied the child being pulled, but the judge awarded her the child. In *Itakura seiyō*, 6, ll, "On the robber who stole five containers," there is a similar story.

1. *Ema,* wooden horse-painting charm, or a picture depicting a horse, was presented to shrines and temples for supplication and recompensation.

4. WITHOUT TWO PARTIES PRESENT THE STOREHOUSE DOES NOT OPEN

This case resembles *Itakura seiyō*, 8, 14, "On the going in and out of the broker."

6. A MEMORY DEVICE TIED TO THE LITTLE FINGER

A similar case can be seen in *T'ang Ying Pi Shih,* no. 134, "Chao Ho redeems the wealth."

7. A MAN WITH A MIND MANIFEST IN SMOKE

1. A similar story of deception, by one Ten'ichi-bō, appears in the novel *Ōoka Seidan.* The famous town magistrate, Ōoka Tadasuke (1677–1751) uncovers the imposter Ten'ichibō, who claimed to be heir to the Tokugawa shōgun, Yoshimune, saying that his mother was a concubine of the shōgun. *Ōoka Seidan* is based on a true story of Genji-bō Kaigyō, the imposter, who is exposed and beheaded. Saikaku's story is purely coincidental.
Tengu is an imaginary being believed to have a long nose, red face, wings and magical powers. He was thought to live deep in the mountains.

8. THEY KNEW THE NAME BUT NOT THE FACE

1. A metaphor meaning entertaining guests in the grand manner.

9. TRANSMITTING THE NOH MASTER'S ART

1. In contrast to the noh performances on stages, this type was performed in living rooms *(zashiki)* of temples and other places.

2. Saigyō (1118–1190) was a poet-priest who traveled to many places in Japan. His poetry collection is titled *Sankashū.*

3. Song about a harlot who lived in the port of Eguchi (in Ōsaka City) and composed poems with Saigyō.

Measure Equivalents

MONEY UNIT

Gold *(kin)*	4 *shu*	= 1 *bu*
	4 *bu*	= 1 *ryo*
Silver *(gin)*	1 *kan*	= 1000 *momme*
Copper *(zeni)*	1 *kan*	= 1000 *mon*

During the Tokugawa Period, copper coins were circulated throughout Japan, silver coins mainly in western Japan (Kyōto-Ōsaka area), and gold coins mainly in Edo (Tōkyō). Gold, silver, and copper were usually exchanged by weight, and the rate fluctuated:

1 *ryo* = 50 to 80 *momme* = 4 to 7 *kamme*

LENGTH

1 *sun*	= 1.2 inches
1 *shaku*	= 0.99 foot
1 *ken*	= 1.99 yards
1 *cho*	= 119 yards
1 *ri*	= 2.44 miles

AREA

1 square *ken* = 3.95 square yards

VOLUME

1 *go* = 0.32 pints

WEIGHT

1 *momme*	= 0.13 ounce
1 *kin*	= 1.32 pounds
1 *kan*	= 8.27 pounds

Index to the Notes

Thomas M. Kondo graduated with M.A. degrees in Japanese literature from Ryukoku University (Kyoto, Japan) and history (University of Hawaii). At present, he teaches Japanese at the University of Hawaii, Kapiolani Community College.

Alfred H. Marks has translated several Japanese modern novels including *Forbidden Colors* and *Thirst for Love* by Mishima Yukio. He is Professor of English at New York State University (New Paltz).

Asian Studies at Hawaii

No. 1   *Bibliography of English Language Sources on Human Ecology, Eastern Malaysia and Brunei.* Compiled by Conrad P. Cotter with the assistance of Shiro Saito. September 1965. Two parts. (Available only from
Paragon Book Gallery, New York.)

No. 2   *Economic Factors in Southeast Asian Social Change.* Edited by Robert
Van Niel. May 1968. Out of print.

No. 3   *East Asian Occasional Papers (1).* Edited by Harry J. Lamley. May
1969.

No. 4   *East Asian Occasional Papers (2).* Edited by Harry J. Lamley. July
1970.

No. 5   *A Survey of Historical Source Materials in Java and Manila.* Robert
Van Niel. February 1971.

No. 6   *Educational Theory in the People's Republic of China: The Report of
Ch'ien Chung-Jui.* Translated by John N. Hawkins. May 1971. Out of
print.

No. 7   *Hai Jui Dismissed from Office.* Wu Han. Translated by C. C. Huang.
June 1972.

No. 8   *Aspects of Vietnamese History.* Edited by Walter F. Vella. March
1973.

No. 9   *Southeast Asian Literatures in Translation: A Preliminary Bibliography.* Philip N. Jenner. March 1973.

No. 10 *Textiles of the Indonesian Archipelago.* Garrett and Bronwen Solyom.
October 1973. Out of print.

No. 11 *British Policy and the Nationalist Movement in Burma, 1917–1937.* Al-
bert D. Moscotti. February 1974.

No. 12 *Aspects of Bengali History and Society.* Edited by Rachel Van M.
Baumer. December 1975.

No. 13 *Nanyang Perspective: Chinese Students in Multiracial Singapore.* Andrew W. Lind. June 1974.

No. 14 *Political Change in the Philippines: Studies of Local Politics preceding Martial Law.* Edited by Benedict J. Kerkvliet. November 1974.

No. 15 *Essays on South India.* Edited by Burton Stein. February 1976.

No. 16 *The* Caurāsī Pad *of Śrī Hit Harivaṁś.* Charles S. J. White. 1977.

No. 17 *An American Teacher in Early Meiji Japan.* Edward R. Beauchamp. June 1976.

No. 18 *Buddhist and Taoist Studies I.* Edited by Michael Saso and David W. Chappell. 1977.

No. 19 *Sumatran Contributions to the Development of Indonesian Literature, 1920–1942.* Alberta Joy Freidus. 1977.

No. 20 *Insulinde: Selected Translations from Dutch Writers of Three Centuries on the Indonesian Archipelago.* Edited by Cornelia N. Moore, 1978.

No. 21 *Regents, Reformers, and Revolutionaries: Indonesian Voices of Colonial Days, Selected Historical Readings, 1899–1949.* Translated, edited, and annotated by Greta O. Wilson, 1978.

No. 22 *The Politics of Inequality: Competition and Control in an Indian Village.* Miriam Sharma. October 1978.

No. 23 *Brokers of Morality: Thai Ethnic Adaptation in a Rural Malaysian Setting.* Louis Golomb. February 1979.

No. 24 *Tales of Japanese Justice.* Ihara Saikaku. Translated by Thomas M. Kondo and Alfred H. Marks. January 1980.

Orders for Asian Studies at Hawaii publications should be directed to The University Press of Hawaii, 2840 Kolowalu Street, Honolulu, Hawaii 96822. Present standing orders will continue to be filled without special notification.